MARY WIBBERLEY

the man at la valaise

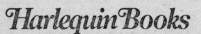

Harlequin Books

TORONTO • LONDON • NEW YORK • AMSTERDAM • SYDNEY • WINNIPEG

Harlequin Presents edition published February 1976
SBN 373-70629-4

Original hard cover edition published in 1973
by Mills & Boon Limited

CHAPTER ONE

AND there it was. Sacha caught a glimpse of the roof of La Valaise before it was hidden again by thick umbrella pines. But it was there all right. She'd made it!

Her lips curved in a smile as she gripped the wheel of the little Citroën more firmly. This was the tricky part of the road, possibly the most difficult she had encountered since Nice airport, where she had hired the car; but it somehow made it all worth while when the red-pantiled roof came into sight, as it just had, and made the tiring plane journey, the hours on the road afterwards, melt away. Sacha wondered if Madame Cassel would be there. Sometimes, if she knew when you were arriving, she would be waiting with cold home-made lemonade, and perhaps a meal of ham and crusty bread and olives.

Sacha reached out for a paper tissue and dabbed her face. It was hot, too hot for late May. The sky had an overbright sheen, as if it might explode into rain, and maybe that would lessen the intolerable heat. Her dress clung damply, stickily to her. Oh, for a cool shower! That was one modern amenity La Valaise boasted—no bath, but a gorgeous, small shower room.

The crumbling high walls at each side of the narrow track seemed to be about to tumble over— but they had been like that for years, ever since Sacha could remember, and her first visit had been eight years ago, at the age of fourteen. And now . . .

And then suddenly the unexpected, the *impossible* happened. She had turned her head slightly to see a plump thrush that had landed on a jutting-out stone atop the wall. When she turned back again, she slammed on her brakes instinctively as a motorbike roared to a stop, slewed sideways across the track, only feet away from the bonnet of the car.

There was an explosive, shattering silence for several moments, and Sacha breathed again. She saw the man get off the motorbike, looked and saw —and kept on looking, because what she was seeing was interesting, to say the least. He was a tall man, over six feet, and well built with it, so that she had a momentary qualm. Dark, very dark, probably because he was so tanned, but he would be dark anyway, wearing faded blue denim shorts, and a matching shirt that was unbuttoned in the heat, bare feet thrust into the very briefest of espadrilles. His legs were long and hairy and muscular, chest and arms equally so, and his face—his face was fascinating. Black hair grew low on his forehead, in a widow's peak. High cheekbones, dark eyes and brows, a wide, almost humorous mouth, a face of strength and power—and he wasn't angry, he seemed in fact to be smiling. The next second her door was opened, and Sacha stepped out to confront the man grinning down at her. She was tall herself, nearly five foot eight, but he towered over her easily as he said in French:

'I am sorry, *mademoiselle,* I hope I didn't frighten you, but I didn't expect to see anyone—you see, this road is private.'

'Yes, I know,' she answered in French, but he broke in:

'You are English?' And he *said* it in English.

'Yes, but how—?' she broke off helplessly, the beginnings of a smile irresistibly breaking through her still face. He laughed, his teeth white against that tan.

'I recognise your accent. There is no mistaking English—no?'

And one thing was certain. He was neither English nor French, and she wondered fleetingly what nationality he was. 'No,' she agreed. 'But I'm sorry —you see, I didn't expect to meet anyone either— I thought this road led only to La Valaise—'

'That is so, then why—' and for a moment she saw something disturbing in his features. Just for a brief second, then it was gone.

'That's where I'm going.' And she smiled again at him. He really was good-looking, in a virile, tough kind of way. Tough, yes, that was the word to describe him. And a faint shiver touched Sacha's spine, but she couldn't have said why.

'There must be some mistake.' And his smile was subdued now. Still there, but toned down, as if . . . 'La Valaise is occupied by my—family and myself.' There had been the faintest pause before family. 'And we have it for the next few weeks, so—' he shrugged, and it was a graceful gesture, but now she was too disturbed to notice, or be impressed.

'No,' she said firmly. 'No. I'm sorry, but I have the letter here—' and she bent her head to fumble in her bag, so that she nearly missed what happened next.

A man's voice shouted: 'Tor, *prinesite mne malen*—' and she looked up startled to see a grey-haired man who had stopped a few feet away, who had come from the direction of the house, and who stood bewildered on that stony dirt road, as if realising . . .

And the man from the motorbike turned and said something, swiftly, *angrily* to him—and the language he spoke was tantalisingly familiar yet elusive. And the older man half turned, his arms going up and out in an almost apologetic gesture as if to say—'But I didn't know—' and then, quickly, quietly, he began to walk back in the direction of La Valaise. The man with the motorbike turned back again to Sacha, and as he did, two thoughts came to her almost simultaneously. That old man had a face that had been vaguely familiar—as if she had seen him before—but once only . . . And this

8

man's name was Tor. What a fascinating name, Tor.

Something had changed. Even as she fumbled again in her bag, the tall man made a gesture as if to say—'it doesn't matter', and he reached out his hand to touch Sacha's arm. 'See,' he said. 'There has been a misunderstanding. Come with me to the house and we will untangle the matter over a drink.' She was compelled to look up at him, for his touch burned like fire on her arm, and she was disturbed by what she saw in his eyes. 'It is a hot day, no?'

And all at once, quite suddenly, Sacha knew she must get away. She didn't know what it was, some deep instinctive warning bell ringing inside her—but her whole body tingled as she said, speaking as casually as she could—and it was suddenly very important that she did speak *casually* to let him see . . .

'Look,' she answered. 'Perhaps I've made a mistake. I've an aunt in Cannes, I'll just go and visit her, and——'

'No,' he said softly, but it stopped her words short. 'I think not. It would not be fair to turn you away after your journey. Come, we will go now, and then afterwards'—again that curiously graceful, indolent shrug—'we will decide. I am so sorry.'

Sacha turned towards the Citroën, and if she had to reverse all the way back down to the road along that stony twisting track, she would do it, for the tingle of alarm was frightening now,

9

more so because of the beauty around them, and the bright sunshine, and the sheer *normality* of birds singing in distant trees. And she looked at the man as her hand touched the door, with its window wound right down to let in the air, and she smiled at him with a great effort. She had thought him attractive before, and he still was, heart-stoppingly so —but there was another quality added now, and she could not have put words to it, but she was frightened. 'I must go,' she said.

The man called Tor moved swiftly, leaned in and took out the keys from the ignition, and held them in his hand, throwing them lightly into the air and catching them again as he said: 'No. Not yet.'

Sacha was resourceful, and she had courage. She had once sent a young thug flying, after seeing him attack and rob an old lady, had hit him with all her young strength and then sat on him until help arrived. But something told her that this man was well out of the young thug class—in a different league altogether. So she faced him, head up, chin tilted defiantly, and said: 'I don't know what your game is—but I'd like my keys back *now*, please.' And she held out her hand, her clear blue eyes gazing into hard slate grey ones.

'Game?' he half smiled, a mere quirk of that wide mouth. 'I am sorry, I do not understand. I merely wish——'

Then Sacha made her first mistake as she

reached out to take the keys he held so casually. He took her hand with his free one, just gently, but firmly, and she felt the strength behind that grasp, and wrenched herself free. Her breast rose and fell with her heightened breathing, and an icy trickle of pure fear ran down her spine, and she turned, holding tight to her handbag, and began to run down the uneven path because she knew now what was to happen, and she was going to get away, come what may, and the main road was only a mile down —could she make it? The walls on either side jogged and fell with her quick running steps, and she wondered if this was all a nightmare, if she was still asleep on the plane . . . Even as she felt herself being caught and held, and she knew it was no dream, it was real, and she kicked out violently, lashed out with her arms as well, to struggle with the dark man.

It was no use. She had known really, but she had had to try. 'Please—do not struggle—you will only hurt yourself. You must come now, don't you know? If only you had not seen—if you had come at another time, not then——' and he stopped, as if he had said too much, as he led her back, up the rough pebble-strewn road, and she stumbled, and his arm tightened round her. Anyone seeing us would think we were lovers, thought Sacha bitterly. Side by side, his arm round her waist, he slowing his long stride to match hers . . . If only that was all it was!

'Take your hands off me,' she breathed, and he did so immediately.

'But if you try and run again, I will not listen. understand?' he asked. They were in sight of the house now, so familiar, so *safe*-looking—it always had been, until now anyway. And she wasn't at all surprised to see another man at the door. As they got closer she saw him properly, and faltered, and the man called Tor whispered: 'It is all right. He is harmless.'

Madame Cassel wouldn't be far away. That was the only thought in Sacha's mind now, the only thing she had to cling to, for the house was never let without her being there to housekeep, and she would make everything all right—she would—she *must*.

'Please go in.' The other man had vanished, and that was a relief, and Sacha's tall companion pushed open the door for her. Feeling as if she were going to her doom she went in, and had to pause to let her eyes adjust to the comparative darkness after the blinding sunlight. The feel of the cool red stone tiles underfoot was reassuring somehow. It *was* La Valaise. There might be strangers there, but the house didn't change.

His voice broke into her thoughts. 'Please sit down. You would like a drink of tea or coffee?' She was thirsty, but a horrible suspicion filled her and she answered quickly, without thinking: 'Only if I make it myself.'

He laughed, and there was nothing sinister there, in the way he threw his head back, the joyous roar of laughter that came out.

'Ah, so I will not drug it? Very well, yes, if you wish. Come,' and he beckoned towards the kitchen, which led off from the large main living room of the house. Sacha went out, and he followed. She was looking round, weighing up, seeing what was changed, but everything looked just as it always had. It was even, she could have sworn, the same bunch of onions hung up on the wall, next to the brightly coloured picture of Mary and Child that had adorned the wall since time immemorial. The walls were rough plaster, blue-washed, a little faded now, and the cooker and cupboards were just as they had always been, solid and old and comfortable-looking. Sacha sighed and looked around, and Tor bent to a cupboard, lifted out a tin and opened it.

'Tea,' he said. 'You English drink tea, yes? You would like that, I think?'

'Yes,' she answered, but before she could move to the kettle he lifted it from the black cooker, went to the tap and filled it.

She watched him, watched his deft quick movements as he lit the gas and put the kettle over the blue flames. 'Where do you come from?' she asked, and she still felt a tingle where his arm had rested at her waist before.

He turned and looked at her and shook his head

faintly. 'Let us drink first,' he answered. 'Then is the time for questions, I think.'

'I want to know now,' she answered. She had seen a large wooden pole resting against a cupboard. Swung hard it would be an effective club, and she wasn't frightened to use it, but how many more men were there? She had already seen two, both apparently now keeping well out of the way. This one had said he was staying there with his 'family'—well, he would, wouldn't he, she reasoned, if he wanted her to go away—wanted everything to appear *normal*. And she was probably right in assuming that the others would stay out of sight for a while anyway. But what if they saw her running away—alone? The older man had been about sixty—and just why did his face haunt her so? And the other had been bald and too fat to run fast. So—Sacha glanced again at the pole, carefully, for even though he was watching the kettle and not her, he was too sharp for her liking. But she didn't want to stay here one minute longer than necessary. The sooner she reached the police, the better—and where had he put her keys? She tried hard to think, then remembered seeing him slip them in the left back pocket of his denim shorts. That was it, then. Knock him out, grab the keys and run, get the car somehow down to the road and drive like the wind to Tante Marie's. And there, safe, she would phone the police and tell them about the madmen at La Valaise . . .

She jumped as he turned and said something. 'I'm sorry?'

'Sugar? Do you have sugar?'

'Er—no, thank you.' She wouldn't be drinking it anyway, so it didn't matter. She put her bag down casually on the working top, next to a bowl of luscious fruit, and turned casually to look at the calendar on the wall. Her hands tightened as she pictured them clasping that lovely wooden weapon. But the moment hadn't come yet. He was looking in her direction as he remarked: 'The water is nearly boiling. You will put the tea in the pot?'

'Y-yes.' And then he turned away, to reach up to a high shelf for cups, and this was the moment. *Now.* Sacha, with a strength born of fear and desperation, picked up the wooden pole and brought it down on his head... Only the crack she heard came from his shoulders, not his head as he turned that split second too soon, and she knew with sudden despair that he had sensed her move.

The next moment the wood was wrenched from her hands and flung to the floor, and she was facing a savagely angry, white-faced man whose left arm hung at his side...

Fear turned her blood to ice, and she gasped and reached out towards the doorway to freedom ... and was caught and flung back against the hard body of the man, who grated: 'So—and you try to make me think you are innocent!' And with that cryptic, completely incomprehensible remark she was pulled into the main living room and shoved.

The next second she was in the big easy chair—the only one. Tor stood in front of her, and she knew better than to move. She looked at him massaging his left shoulder with his right hand, and the fear was gradually easing away because she knew at that moment that if he had been going to strike her he would have already done so in those few seconds of white-hot anger in the kitchen.

'Now,' he said, 'you will tell me *who* you are and where you come from—and it will be the truth. Where is your passport?'

'In my bag, in the kitchen,' and she ran her tongue over her lips, which were very dry—and the air was hotter than ever. Without a word he went out, came back with her cream straw bag and flung it on her knee. 'Open it and take out your passport—nothing else. You understand me?'

Without a word, Sacha opened her bag. Her only chance of getting away from here was to keep as calm and sensible as possible. She handed him the passport and watched him read it, glancing quickly from her to the photograph as if to compare the image with the reality.

'It says here you are a journalist,' he looked down at her and she stirred uneasily. There was something in his tone she didn't like.

'Yes, but it's only on a—' 'local paper,' she had been going to say, but he didn't let her finish.

'So you wish us to think you come on holiday?'

Those slate grey eyes were still angry, and something else besides. They had a dangerous light in them, and she began to feel afraid again. What was going on?

'Yes. I have Madame Cassel's letter here——'

'Never mind that. Turn your bag out, please—on to the floor.'

A glint of defiance sparked within Sacha. 'No! Who the hell are you?' she demanded.

'I think you already know. Now, are you going to open your bag, or shall I?'

'There's nothing in it to interest you,' she answered.

'Good. Then it will not take a moment. Now—please.' The last word, so softly spoken, had a suggestion of menace.

Sacha opened her bag and tipped its contents to the floor. Plane tickets, receipt for the car, folded letter, driving licence, small packet of aspirins and several items of make-up lay scattered in a small heap on the red stone-tiled floor.

'That is all?' he queried.

For answer she opened the bag to its fullest extent and held it up so that he could see the cream-coloured lining.

'You may put everything back.'

Her head began to throb, a mixture of fear, anger and the heat combining to give her a terrific headache. She pushed everything back, and her fingers were beginning to tremble. She opened the carton of aspirins and took out two, avoiding his eyes.

'What are you doing?' his voice cut in before she could put them to her mouth.

'I have a headache,' she answered, and looked up at him. 'I'm taking two aspirins. Do you mind?'

He nodded, and she saw a muscle work in his hard jaw. He gave her a slight brief smile. 'Perhaps it does not hurt as much as my shoulder,' he commented softly. 'Come, we will finish making that tea. You go first. I prefer to have you where I can see you.'

He stood in the doorway and watched her fill the teapot with boiling water. And she knew without even watching him that he was like a coiled spring, waiting for one wrong move from her.

'There is fresh lemon juice only—no milk.'

'It will do.' She poured out two beakers of strong fresh tea and added lemon juice from the small blue jug.

'We will drink in here. Put the cups on the table.'

She did so and he pulled up a chair opposite her at the scrubbed wooden table and shook out a packet of Gauloises from the pocket of his shorts. 'You would like a cigarette?' he asked.

'I don't smoke.' She sipped the hot refreshing tea and swallowed the aspirins, and watched him. What was happening? Sacha felt more bewildered than she had ever done before in her life. She had longed to arrive here for three quiet weeks of painting and sunbathing and swimming, and the chance to get Nigel out of her system once and for all—and now, suddenly, she wanted nothing more than to get as far away as possible. Tante Marie's small neat flat on the outskirts of Cannes now seemed a haven, an unbelievably wonderful place to be. And she had promised to visit her in a day or so, as always—but now that possibility seemed frighteningly remote.

'Please,' she said suddenly. '*Please* tell me why you are k-keeping me here? I've done nothing—I just c-came here for a holiday.' And tears sprang to her eyes. They were partly caused by the very hot tea she had just swallowed, but he wouldn't know that, and it might help . . .

His face softened slightly. He tapped ash from the end of the Gauloise into the glass ashtray on the table. The strong aromatic, unmistakable odour of French tobacco filled the room. 'I can almost believe you,' he said after a moment. 'I would *like* to believe you, for it is very inconvenient to have you here. But I can take no chances. You shall have your holiday in this house—in a few days. Until then you will stay here as my guest.'

She went utterly cold. For a few moments she literally could not speak. Then, when she found her tongue, she whispered: 'Why—why?'

'If as I think, you already know, then I need not tell you. And if you do not, better you stay that way,' was the cryptic answer.

'No,' she shook her head, and real tears were not far away, for she was tired and hungry, and it was all too much to take, so soon after that last bitter quarrel with Nigel ... 'I know nothing. Honestly. Madame Cassel will vouch for me. I come here every year with my father in July. This year I've come earlier——' she had been about to say 'alone', but a faint idea stirred and stopped her just in time, 'Madame Cassel will tell you I speak the truth. Where is she?'

He smiled at her. 'She is gone to stay with her daughter in Fréjus——'

'No—she never leaves here when anyone comes——' then she stopped. He could perhaps have read her thoughts, for he shook his head gently.

'We have not harmed her. She is truly in Fréjus, and quite well.'

Sacha looked down at her hands curled round the beaker. The headache was worse now, perhaps because of what she was hearing. But she had to go on, *had* to ask. 'But she wouldn't leave here when she was expecting guests——'

'She wrote to those who were due this month—presumably you—to cancel the booking owing to her "illness"——' Tor grinned suddenly. 'So—you tell me you did not receive a letter from her?'

She shook her head. 'No. Only the one confirming my—our visit. I don't understand——'

'It is quite simple.' His long brown finger traced

a pattern in a drop of spilt tea, and Sacha watched it as if mesmerised. 'I told her that I was on my honeymoon, and that we did not wish to be "looked after" or disturbed in any way, and then I gave her a lot of money—and her peasant soul was satisfied. The French are very romantic, as well as practical.'

'Are you on your honeymoon?'

He grinned again, and Sacha, despite herself, was fascinated. He had the most extraordinarily attractive face when he did that, and even his grey eyes lost some of their hardness. 'What do you think?' he asked.

'No. Not with those two men here as well——' she faltered. It might have been better if a woman had been there. Suddenly realisation washed over Sacha. What had he said? He was going to keep her here for a few days—she stood agitatedly and went to the window to lean against it, and press her burning forehead to the cool pane. What was she to do?

'Is your head still hurting?' His voice came suddenly, surprisingly.

'Yes.' She closed her eyes. She must not admit to being frightened—and yet what chance had she against three men? The older one had looked kind, almost gentle—but the bald one—she began to shiver helplessly, then felt Tor's hand on her arm, touching lightly. And he said: 'You will come to no harm while you are here. But you must do as you are told.' Sacha wanted so much to believe him, but she couldn't. She half turned, and had to look up, and he took his hand away.

'But why—why?' she begged.

He looked down at her for a few seconds in silence. 'Because you have seen—by accident—what you should not have seen. That is why. For even if all you say is true, and I let you go now, how do I know who you might talk to?'

'I promise I won't say a word—' she began, but he shook his head.

'No. It is too important for that. You came to stay—and so you will, but for a few days you will have others here as well—'

'My father's coming tonight,' she lied desperately. For a moment that stopped him. Then he gave that graceful shrug.

'And if he does, he will be made very welcome,' and a slight cynical smile touched his mouth. 'But I think you do not speak the truth. Why?'

'You'll see, won't you?' she answered defiantly, but she couldn't meet his eyes. He tilted her chin so that she was forced to.

'Perhaps, yes,' he agreed. 'You look tired. Do you wish to shower? I will have your cases brought from the car now. Wait here.' And as he went out she heard keys jingle in his hand. He called up the stairs, but she stayed where she was. Even with one arm out of action, this man was more than a match for her, she knew. So she listened—and suddenly she knew what language he spoke. The knowledge

22

was even more disquieting. When he came back she was sitting down again.

'He won't be a minute,' he said. 'Do you wish to eat?'

'Have you got caviar?' she asked.

'Ah!' he sat down opposite to her. 'So you know. You speak Russian?'

'No.' That was true, but she had recognised it, and perhaps he wouldn't believe her anyway.

He nodded. 'But even so, we must be careful what we say, eh?' But Sacha wasn't listening. She had made a mistake in admitting she knew his nationality. She should have guessed before, for he had the true Slavic features, the high cheekbones and deep-set eyes and ready smile of his race. And she knew she had to get away from there, now more than ever, and she wouldn't do it by letting him see how frightened she was. She must, she absolutely *must*, appear to be accepting her fate. Later, safely alone in her room, she would be able to think about it.

Gradually, not overdoing it, she made herself appear to relax with him. There was tea left in the pot. As she heard the other man come back through the front door, she asked: 'May I have another cup of tea—and some food? I bought some in Nice—in the carrier bag. I'm awfully hungry.'

Tor stood up. 'Yes. Wait here,' and he came back with the plastic shopper. She heard heavy footsteps going up the stairs from the living room, and she breathed again. There was something about the bald man that had made her flesh creep, even in those few seconds outside.

She had bought a long French loaf, some sweet ham and cheese, and she was hungry enough to eat a hunk of cheese on its own, but she had to wait as he set the food out on the table, checking everything in the bag before he said: 'Good. But first, why do you not wash? There is a good shower upstairs.'

'I know,' she answered. 'I've been here before, remember?' she kept her tone light, but it was an effort. 'I'll go up now. Where are my cases?'

'In there. Come, I will carry them up for you.' She wondered how he would manage, with his left arm. Not that she really cared. All she *really* cared about was leaving, and as soon as possible, and if she had to leave all her luggage behind, she would.

'This way,' he had to nod, his hands too full to point. One case in his left hand, the lighter of the two, the other in his right. Yet still he was like a coiled spring, ready to move in a second—frightening.

The room was at the front of the house, one she had often slept in, and because the faint lavender scent on the bedding lingered, it brought the memories flooding back, so that Sacha stood still by the twin beds for a moment. Never had she dreamed of *this*, yet it was happening now—and for how long would it go on? She turned to the man who stood just inside the door, and something of her emotions must have shown on her face, for his eyes narrowed.

'What is the matter?' he asked. His English was good, but that heavy accent was there, that unmistakable intonation she should have recognised immediately, but had not—and it wouldn't have done her any good if she had. She shook her head.

'Nothing. Is this where I am sleeping?'

'Yes. You know where the shower is—next door to here?'

'Of course.' She straightened up and looked at him. 'And do you intend to stay while I get ready for it?'

The smile transformed the hard planes of his tanned face, and made him appear even more darkly attractive and virile. Sacha was in no mood to appreciate these finer points. Fear still nagged at her, and trying to hide it was difficult—but she was determined to do so, for she knew it would help her. 'No,' he answered, 'of course not. But I warn you not to try and escape again. There is only one small window—too small for you to try and climb out——'

'I thought I was your "guest"?' she queried, and tilted her chin. 'A guest would hardly try to escape, would she?'

He turned, hand on the door, said: 'Of course not. Forgive me.' And he inclined his head in a small bow that was very Russian. His dark eyes, shadowed in that room, because of where he stood, were as black as rain-washed pebbles, but they glinted with a strange expression as he added softly: 'You are most beautiful when you are angry —and even when you are not.' And then he was gone, and Sacha stood very still, disturbed by his words. Who was he, this strange Russian? And, more worrying still—what were he and his companions doing at La Valaise? They were alien there in more ways than one. Still shaken, Sacha bent to click open her case, and her hands had a fine tremor that try as she might, she could not dispel.

CHAPTER TWO

SACHA saw no one either before or after her refreshing shower, but to be on the safe side, she bolted the bedroom door on her return. It was surprising how much better she felt, as if in washing away the fatigue of travel, some of the fears had gone as well.

Sitting on the bed, facing the mirror on the huge ancient wardrobe, she brushed her dark silky hair back and caught it in a red ribbon. Her eyes looked back at her from the fly-specked glass, and she wondered what the dark Russian had read in them. Then she remembered his compliment, so casually spoken, almost as if he meant it—and her mouth tightened rebelliously. The less she listened to things like that, the better. She needed all her wits about her—and *now*—and she wouldn't have if she was going to get girlish flutters every time a big attractive man looked at her in that way he had.

Sacha's eyes were a clear light blue, the shade more attractive because of the dark sooty lashes and brows that nature had given her. A slightly snub neat nose, wide mouth with gentle curve to it that was essentially feminine, she knew she was attractive—she had been told so often enough—but the clear blue of those eyes had lately been shadowed.

It had been so wonderful meeting Nigel, knowing the strong instant attraction had been mutual. Everything had been marvellous and utterly perfect for three months—until that day, that *awful* day only weeks before when the phone call had shattered her life. Just eight words, spoken in an anonymous, husky voice: 'Do you know your boyfriend is married?' That was all—but the shock had been too great for her even to answer. For she had known, with a deep sure feminine instinct, that the words were true.

Sacha paused, the lipstick half way to her mouth, as she recalled the scenes afterwards, the pleading from Nigel: 'But I wanted to tell you—it's all over anyway, the marriage, I mean, Sacha—I'd divorce her if I could...' The excuses she had heard so often before, when friends were pouring their hearts out—words she had never expected to hear herself, because she considered that she was too sensible to be fooled. And to think that she had even considered bringing Nigel down here! Sacha went cold at the thought. Yes, he might have been here with her now, with Madame Cassel as chaperone—but for that phone call.

She took a deep breath, smoothed the colour on quickly and stood up, looking down at her cases. Then, putting all those disturbing thoughts out of her mind, she bent and locked them and put the keys in her bag. She had no thought to leave them for foreign fingers to pry into her belongings—and she couldn't take them with her when she left, which would be soon—very soon, if she had her way . . .

Silence. The house had an uncanny air of quiet about it as she went down the stairs, holding tightly to the wooden rail, for it was suddenly dark, black with swollen clouds racing overhead, and the Mediterranean night which had come quickly. A light glowed in the living room, and another from the kitchen, and she walked across to it and went in.

The food she had brought was gone from the table. In its place were four plates set, and cutlery, and the man called Tor turned from the stove, and she saw the tea towel he wore round his middle like an apron, and suppressed a laugh that might have been a sob . . .

'Good, you are ready. I am preparing soup. You would like some?' and he cocked a thick dark eyebrow at her.

Sacha smelt the delicious aroma at the same moment that she asked: 'Where is my food?'

'Ah! See, I have put it away in the cold place——' he pointed, 'there are too many flies in here. But you will have soup first?' And then he added, quite straight-faced: 'I shall have it with you, so that you will know it is not drugged.'

She sat down. 'Where are the other two men?' she asked. She tried to make it sound casual, as if it didn't really matter, but it did. If they were far

29

away she might have a chance now, or at least, soon.

'Gone for a walk. It is dark now, you see.' As if that explained something, she thought, and wondered again. But hunger was the paramount emotion at the moment, and without something inside her she would be too weak to escape anyway . . .

'Oh, I see. It's going to rain, isn't it?'

'I think so, yes, soon.' He had turned to look out of the window, and on turning back, asked: 'Will you butter bread for me?'

'Yes. Where is it?' As she stood up, she noticed that the wooden pole was gone. Of course . . . An unwilling smile curved her lips. He would be a fool to leave it there, for her to have another go . . . which made what happened later all the more surprising, in retrospect.

His arm was still stiff, that was obvious by the way he used it when ladling out the thick hot brown soup into bowls. Sacha pushed the crusty bread to the middle of the table. A pang of what might have been regret for her action made her say, before she could think about it: 'Does your shoulder hurt much?'

He paused in what he was doing. 'Yes. Why do you ask?'

She swallowed. 'I didn't mean to—I wouldn't—I'm sorry it hurts,' she blurted out abruptly, horrified at her own apology, but quite unable to help herself.

He finished ladling the soup, returned the huge

black pan to the stove before sitting down at the table. Then he looked at her. 'If a man had done what you did,' he said, picking up his spoon, 'I would probably have killed him.'

Sacha was silent. She knew he spoke the truth, and a cold wave seemed to sweep down her body from head to toe. What was he, this man? *Who* was he?

She bent to the soup, hoping that the chill feeling would go in the warmth rising up from the grey earthenware bowl. She picked up a piece of the crusty bread and bit into it. It wasn't her own loaf, but a similar one, and there was grape cheese on the table, and a bowl of shiny fat olives waiting to be eaten.

She was on edge now, and waiting for the other two men to come back. She wondered if her car was still where she had left it, but doubted it. She stole a glance at the man across the table from her. He ate his food quickly, and seemed quite relaxed. Suddenly he looked up and caught her eye.

'Did I frighten you when I said that?' he asked her.

Sacha shook her head. 'No,' she lied.

'Good. I do not mean to. I spoke only the truth. You must not be frightened of me or my comrades. We mean you no harm at all.'

'How do I know that?' she queried, with an attempt at lightness.

'Because I am the boss here—and I do not fight

women,' he answered, and he cut himself a wedge of the creamy cheese, and grinned at her. 'My name is Nikolai Torlenkov. I am always called Tor. And you are Miss Sacha Donnelly——' her name sounded completely foreign on his tongue, and he made 'Sacha' sound very Russian, and new. 'I will call you Sacha, if I may?' And there was a polite questioning tilt to his face as he said it.

'I don't have much choice, do I?' she answered softly, not bitterly.

'It is only for a few days, very few, that you must stay with us—but if you do not permit me to call you by name, then I shall not do so.'

He had managed to make her feel very naïve in those few words. Sacha was annoyed with herself for the feeling, and answered: 'Call me Sacha if you wish. What are the other two called?'

'The younger one—the one who alarmed you—is Janos. The older man is'—he seemed to hesitate —'called Serge.'

'I see. Shouldn't they be back soon?'

'Yes. Soon.' He shrugged then looked at the watch on his wrist. It was very flat, black-faced, set in heavy silver on a wide silver band, and Sacha could see that it was nearly eight. The soup was delicious, full of small chunks of meat and diced vegetables—and very filling. She pushed her plate away, and began to put a plan together as she yawned.

'Oh, excuse me! I'm so tired,' she admitted, with

a shy smile at the man opposite her.

He took her plate. 'You have come from England today?'

'Yes.' And if she had been tired before her shower, it was no longer true, but she wasn't going to admit it. Let him think she was exhausted and he wouldn't watch her so keenly. 'Travelling always makes me sleepy—and the journey from the airport is tiring too. I was looking forward to an early night,' and she leaned forward to pick up cheese and olives so that he wouldn't be able to see her face.

'You shall have one. Of course.' He had an odd way of speaking, of cutting short his sentences, and it had a charm about it, just as everything did about him, and Sacha wondered why she should find it so, when he and the other men were so obviously up to no good at La Valaise. She went cold at that thought. Suppose they were criminals? Smugglers—or worse? La Valaise was sufficiently isolated to appeal to a gang who needed time, and privacy, and she had only this man's word that Madame Cassel was all right. Dear old Madame Cassel who was always there to welcome visitors—and who would either sleep at the house itself, or at her own little cottage a mere few hundred yards away—and Sacha's eyes widened at the remembrance of that. Of course! Why hadn't she thought of *that* before! She had to get to the little house to *see*—to reassure herself that the old woman wasn't lying tied up—

or—or—but Sacha's mind refused to carry her any further.

It was later that the chance came. The two men had returned from their walk, and Sacha had seen them both close to, properly, and been more bemused than ever. The one named Janos was completely bald, fat, about fifty with icy cold blue eyes and no expression on his face. He had bowed at Sacha, abruptly, curtly, when he came in, and she had had to fight to keep an expression of disinterested calm on her face. Tor said to her: 'Janos does not speak English, Sacha——' and then Serge had entered, and he was different again, so different that Sacha found herself responding to that gentle smile on a worn tired face of a man who must have been over sixty, grey-haired and too thin, dark brown eyes deep set in his slightly tanned face. He came forward, unlike Janos, and held out a thin hand whose skin was as dry as paper. Then he said something briefly to Tor, who told Sacha: 'Serge says he is sorry you have had a bad start to your holiday.'

'Thank you.' She smiled back, but could say no more. For what was there to say? As the two men sat down at the table, Sacha stood up and looked at Tor. What now? Several vague plans wreathed through her mind, all equally amorphous, all waiting for something to trigger them off into something positive—but she would wait and be patient. That was something her journalistic training had prepared her for, and it was beginning to assert itself more and more with each hour that passed; to help her in an odd way.

It was clear that Tor didn't want her to stay in the kitchen now that the men had returned. He indicated the living room, said something to the others and took Sacha's arm.

'Come. They will eat now.' And then, in the other room, he looked at her. 'You are tired—yes?'

'Yes——' sudden inspiration came. 'But I want to go for a walk first—I can't sleep if I don't have a walk before bedtime.' She held her breath as she waited for his answer. Would it work?

He shrugged. 'If you wish. But it is cooler now. You have a coat?'

Her heart leapt—but no excitement must show, nothing to give her away. She had changed after her shower into blue jeans and blue sweater, the darkest clothes she had—and she had a red jacket upstairs—and it was to be hoped that it didn't show up too much in the dark outside—for if her chance came, and she made a run for it, the less he could see the better.

'I'll go up and find one.' She could smile at him now. 'I suppose you'll be coming with me on this walk?'

'You think I would let you go alone?' he grinned suddenly. 'On such a dark night? Better not, eh? You do not know who you might meet.'

He was being humorous, so she smiled, because

she didn't intend to do anything to antagonise him, and the retort that she could hardly be worse off than she was remained unspoken.

A few minutes later he was holding open the front door of the house for her. He had donned a thin white sweater, and Sacha smiled to herself. She could see *him* in the dark with no difficulty, none at all.

She turned towards Madame Cassel's cottage before he could choose a direction. The gardens were so different at night, dark and shadowy—if she had been there alone, she wouldn't have come out on her own, but would have had the doors safely bolted. Now was different. She was quite prepared to walk miles through the ghostly grey darkness if she could manage to escape him. And she wouldn't be frightened at all, only relieved. The trees were black and silent, the sky still cloud-swollen, and she breathed deeply of the sharp night air, faintly and deliciously scented with eucalyptus and pine mingled. Grass rustled underfoot, and somewhere from one of the trees came a faint creak as the wood settled. Sacha shivered, glad of her coat, and Tor said: 'It is perhaps too cold for you?'

'No,' she answered. 'I heard a sound—I—I'm glad you're with me. It's a bit spooky in the dark.'

He laughed softly. 'Spooky? What is that?'

'Well, you know—ghostly—frightening,' she hid a grin, even though he wouldn't have been able to see it. Let him think she was too *timid* to run away

36

even if she could! He was very big beside her, and it made her uncomfortably aware of the fragility of her position. To cover up, to keep everything normal, she asked: 'How long have you been here—or is that a secret?' Her tone was perfectly casual, as if she were making polite conversation.

'A few days only. Tell me, Sacha, what part of England do you come from?'

So he didn't want to answer any questions. Not surprising, she knew. Criminals were very wary of telling their life stories to all and sundry—and yet something bothered her. He didn't *act* like a criminal—not that Sacha had had many encounters with any. But there was an air of assured confidence—almost arrogance—about him that sat oddly on her preconceived notion of how a crook should behave. Yet she didn't know, not at all.

'I live near Birmingham, in a place called Walsall,' she answered. 'Do you know it?'

They were nearly there now, and he was certainly showing no signs of alarm, or appearing to want to leave . . . and she could see the house now, dark and shuttered and silent, and she caught her breath. She was going to have to be very clever.

'No, alas, I have never been to your country—but one day I will, for I like the English,' he answered.

Oh, do you? thought Sacha. And do you kidnap all the English girls you see? But the words couldn't be said aloud, for she was going to be nice to him at all costs, despite her nagging fears.

'I'm afraid you won't find it as warm as here,' she said. 'But then you get it pretty cold in Russia at times, don't you?'

'At times, yes,' he agreed solemnly. Then, quite suddenly, he stopped, and his hand on her arm stopped Sacha too. 'Wait,' he said quietly, and she froze in her tracks.

'What—' she breathed.

'Ssh, a noise. Listen.' They were in the shadows of a huge tree, and the darkness was all around them, pressing in on them, and all Sacha could hear was Tor breathing, and the faint dry rustle of the leaves in the trees, but a tingle of fear touched her spine with an icy finger and she caught her breath.

Then, softly, he laughed. 'Ah no! I forgot!'

'Tell me—' she began.

'Come, I will show,' and he took her arm and led her to the back of Madame Cassel's tiny cottage— and Sacha saw the faint fat shapes on the ground, and the slight movements—and her knees went weak with relief.

'The hens!' she said. 'I forgot the hens!' She turned wide eyes to the man at her side. 'But who's feeding them? Madame Cassel wouldn't leave them.' She should have remembered; the know-ledge had been nagging at her mind before.

'I am,' he answered, and his voice held laughter. 'And in return we can have the eggs—which is why we eat them at every meal. Do you know some good new ways of cooking them?'

'Yes—but we didn't have any with the soup,' she pointed out.

'No, but we will have omelettes for supper. You like that?'

Sacha repressed a shudder. Omelettes for *supper*! What a thought.

'No, thank you. Just a drink will do me.' If I'm there, she added silently. If . . .

They walked on, past the darkened hen-coop from inside which faint flutterings and contented cluckings could be heard as some of the birds settled themselves down for the night. The air was heavy and scented, and had gone surprisingly warmer so that Sacha slipped off her jacket and put it over her arm. They were at the edge of the gardens now, and stopped, for the sea was in the distance, and further still, very clear and beautiful in the still night air, could be seen a string of lights along the road, like a diamond necklace set on a bed of black velvet, glistening and glittering in the night, almost competing with the few faint stars that could be seen through cloud. Sacha stood still and drew her breath in sharply. The sight of the sea never failed to move her, and at night it was even more breathtakingly beautiful and mysterious. Faintly a yacht moved, miles away, well lit, and she wondered who was aboard her, and if they were having a party, and caught her breath at the thought, and shivered helplessly.

'You are cold. We will return.' Tor spoke softly. She had almost managed to forget him. Almost ...

'No, I'm not cold. I'm just looking at that boat,' and she pointed her arm and her jacket slid to the ground. Before she could pick it up, he had bent and done so, but he didn't give it to her, and she said: 'It's all right——'

'No, I will carry it for you—or do you want it on?'

'No, thanks.' There was something in the air that had nothing to do with the night, or the background; an unknown, tingling quality that made her heartbeats quicken as she became suddenly, meltingly aware of Tor as a man—and a devastatingly attractive one at that.

She moved quickly away, disturbed at his nearness. What mad impulse had possessed her to come out like this, with him? Then she remembered. It was to make sure that Madame Cassel was not being held prisoner in her own cottage—and also to try to get away.

She was looking away from him now, out to the calm soothing sea again. What chance had she to escape this man? Sacha was healthy and strong, but she knew with a deep certainty that he was in every way infinitely stronger. It was in the way he stood, the muscular powerful build of him, even in the arrogant angle of his head and chin, a challenging tilt, as if to say: 'Try anything at your own risk.'

If Sacha was to get away, then it would have to be by cunning and stealth. And *that* prospect didn't seem as if it would be easy either. The man was no fool, that much was already quite obvious—and another thing, he was watching her all the time . . .

Sacha gave a deep sigh of despair and turned round, not looking at him. Better to wait until she was safely alone in her bedroom before she began to think. The window wasn't too high from the ground—and it was grass underneath, not paving . . .

'What is the matter?' his voice brought her back to the present, and she looked up, startled.

'Nothing. I was just thinking how different it would have been, if——' and she paused, as if wondering if she had said too much. Anything to keep him from guessing the *real* trend of her thoughts . . .

'Yes, I know. I regret very much. But it is not for long. Soon——' she saw him shrug, and she wanted to shout:

'Stop doing that!' but she had to bite her lip instead.

'Soon, it will be yours again. In a few days.'

Sacha didn't answer. It was no use. She didn't believe him any more. She didn't know what to believe about anything. What was happening was so unbelievable and fantastic as to be completely outside her knowledge of life. Things like this didn't happen to people you *knew*. They happened in newspapers, something to be discussed over the coffee and marmalade at the breakfast table, or perhaps at work, and then forgotten.

Even in the office they would think she had gone mad if she ever came in with a story like this. The editor was used to dealing with local JPs being fined for parking without lights, eight-foot-tall wall-flowers being grown in window boxes, or what the beauty queen's mother told our correspondent about my Dawn's hobbies—but never *this*.

'So you say. But if I don't phone my father to-night he will be very worried—and send the police here.' It was a brave attempt at a lie, and she said it as convincingly as she could—and then knew her mistake as Tor took hold of her arms and turned her to face him, and said, very softly:

'But your father is coming here himself, yes?'

She looked up at him, panic flaring in her eyes. What on earth had possessed her to say such a ridiculous thing?

'Yes—that is—but not for a day. I have to phone him—h-he's in Paris tonight and flying to Nice to-morrow. I have to call him to check what time h-he arrives.' If only she *could* get to a phone . . .

'Ah, I see. Then I will phone for you. Give me his number——' he began.

'No! What would he think if a man spoke——' his touch on her arms was one of fire. His fingers burned and tingled, and she wanted to move away —and yet, in a way, she didn't. It was most odd.

'Ah, but I would say I was Madame Cassel's nephew, and that you had asked me to call because you were very tired——'

'No. It won't do, he'll expect to hear me——'

'You are lying, Sacha,' he said, and he shook her gently. 'You try hard, but I know a lie when I hear it. Ah, I do not blame you, for——'

'Don't touch me!' If he didn't let go of her she would scream, because she couldn't bear it any more.

Slowly, almost, it seemed, reluctantly, he released her. 'Am I offensive to you?' he asked, curious. 'Do you think I will hurt you?' He was asking it quite seriously now.

Sacha tried to breathe calmly. She had to—she *must* keep calm above all else. 'It's just—I d-don't like people touching me,' she answered, 'that's all.'

In the darkness she saw the white gleam of his teeth as he smiled. 'Ah, I see. You English do not like people to touch—yes, yes, I remember—but we Russians, we are not like that, perhaps?'

'Perhaps. I don't know. Hadn't we better go back to the house?'

'If you wish. Do you want your coat——' but even as he said it, the rain started, and they both looked up, startled. It wasn't like English rain, sharp and stinging, it was soft, almost warm, and the drops were huge, so that they splashed caressingly and gently on Sacha's upturned face.

'Oh, marvellous——' and then she remembered.

'My hair!' she exclaimed. Tor took her hand.

'Come.' He was laughing, and suddenly she didn't mind him holding her hand as they began to run towards the dark silent cottage with its sheltering doorway. He pulled her into that dark porch, smelling faintly of garlic and herbs. And he said: 'What is the matter with your hair?'

She shook her head, laughing as well, because the rain was a soft balm that had brought magical release from the tension of those few moments ago. 'I had it set yesterday—and I want it to last a while —and it won't if I get it soaked as soon as I arrive.' She didn't know why she was telling him this.

'Ah, yes, I see.' He reached his hand out and stroked the silky softness. 'It is beautiful—like you, Sacha.' And she lifted her face and shook her head from side to side, gently protesting.

'No,' she said. 'No—you——' but her next words were lost as the night was blotted out by Tor's head. He had her coat, and he was sliding it round her shoulders, but why was he leaning so close? He didn't have to come so . . . His lips were cool with that rain, and very gentle, and Sacha melted into them, and then, horrified, gasped and tried to pull herself free. But she could not, his hands were on her shoulders, she could feel the warmth of them through the thin material of the red jacket.

Tor brushed his lips against her cheek, then her hair, as she turned vainly, struggling like a trapped bird in a net. 'No!' she managed, and he laughed.

'Why not? Do you English not like kissing either? I do not think that I wish to come to your country after all.' His voice was light with amusement. That was what it had been to him, a momentary impulse, nearness in the rain to add to the temptation—and the result a kiss, a harmless brief embrace. And that was all. But Sacha's heartbeat was erratic, and her lips ached from the touch, and it made her obscurely angry, almost frightened—of herself as well as this tall impudent stranger.

She fought to keep her breathing steady. The doorway was dark, so dark that even the rain-shadowed trees seemed almost light and welcoming. She leaned against the rough stone wall behind her, and the door was to her left, and her scattered wits were gradually coming back to her. The rain was heavier now, rich and warm and pattering to the ground to be instantly blotted up by the parched earth, and it made that dark doorway an inevitable haven. And yet for how long? Sacha moved slightly, the stone rough on her hand, and Tor said: 'You have beautiful lips. I like kissing you. Why do you struggle so?'

'Don't be stupid!' she retorted. 'Why should I let *you*, a perfect stranger, kiss me just because you want to?' She was surprised at his impudence— more, she was disturbed. She had never met a man like him—a *criminal*, up to no good, she had to remind herself immediately afterwards.

'No, you are right,' he agreed gravely. 'It was

very bad of me. I apologise very humbly, Miss Sacha Donnelly,' and he bowed slightly, as well as he could in that small dark space.

Sacha fought the unreasoning flare of anger his words induced in her. She must not let him have this effect on her; it was essential to keep calm if she was to leave soon, for he was far too shrewd for her liking. And yet her hand tingled with the urge to slap him, to wipe that mocking air from him.

She turned away, clenching her fists to stop the wish becoming the deed, and bit back the words she wanted so much to say. She saw him glance down at her as if puzzled, but knew he could see very little in the darkness. Very stealthily, with her left hand, she reached out and along to feel the door handle—to see if the door would open— though what she would do if it did, she had not yet decided. Suddenly his hand clamped down on hers, as she was just touching the door latch, and he let his breath out in an explosive sigh.

'So! Tell me what you are doing, please.'

Sacha wrenched her hand free from his larger one. 'Nothing!' she said. 'I couldn't remember which way the door opened.' Even to her own ears it sounded a pretty feeble excuse, and he began to laugh.

'No, I think not. Still you do not trust me, eh? Now I know why you walk so quickly this way— you think that perhaps the old lady is inside?' And at her silent seething, he touched her cheek. 'Tell me.'

That slight touch, almost a caress, was the spark that lit the fuse of Sacha's temper. She knocked his hand away and turned on him angrily. 'Keep your dirty paws off me!' she stormed. 'Stop touching me all the time! I've told you I don't like it. Who the hell do you think you are?'

He gave an almost silent, almost invisible whistle. 'Ah, that is better. This is you again, yes? You were so quiet—I thought perhaps you were plotting something,' he said.

His words were a shock. Was that how she had seemed? If so it was just as well she had exploded now. It was a sobering thought—but he was even cleverer than she had suspected. She was so shaken that his words had the effect of temporarily silencing her while she thought furiously what on earth to do next.

His next words were even more of a surprise. He felt in his pocket and she heard the jingle of keys and wondered briefly, ridiculously, if he was going to give her her car keys back. But then he was pushing one in the door. 'You would like to see for yourself that I have not got Madame Cassel tied up and gagged? Go in, please.' The door opened, the light clicked on, and Sacha swallowed hard, blinking in that sudden glare of yellow flooding out.

She stayed rooted to the spot, and Tor clicked his teeth impatiently.

'You are going to stand there?'

'Why—why did she give you her keys?' Sacha asked in a faint voice. Now the opportunity had come for her to actually see for herself, doubt filled her.

'So that I might come in for the hens' food—also to feed the goldfish.' He smiled crookedly in that yellow light. 'Now, please, are you going to look or not?'

Sacha took a deep breath and made up her mind. 'Yes,' she answered.

It took only minutes to look through the tiny house and reassure herself that no living creature was there—or dead one, for that matter. He stood waiting by the door for her, and was careful not to touch her as she passed him to go out. He switched off the light and locked the door again, and the darkness was made more intense because of that brief time of light. The rain was no less heavy, but Sacha had had enough of standing in shady doorways with this big unpredictable man. She lifted her coat and pulled it over her head. 'I'm going back to La Valaise,' she said, then added, reluctantly: 'Do you want to come under my coat?'

'Ay-ay!' he gave a shocked exclamation. 'Do you think I would dare? No, for I do not want to have my eyes scratched out if I should touch you by accident!'

Without a word, Sacha set off walking fast. She could not imagine the shock in store for her at the house.

The men had gone when they went in. The scent of tobacco lingered in the air, and she had seen a light from one of the bedrooms, the largest, as she ran up the path to the front door—but that was all. The plates were cleared and washed, and the kitchen was neat and tidy. Sacha stood in the living room and waited to be told what to do. Tor went into the kitchen and beckoned her.

'Please,' he said. 'You wish for a drink? Some food?'

Perhaps it would be a good idea to eat. She would need energy for that long walk she was going to take. So she smiled. 'I'll have some of my ham with bread,' she answered. 'Do you want some?'

'No, I will have an omelette, thank you.' He pulled off the white sweater and flung it on a chair. Rain glistened on his face and hair and he wiped his hand across his chin and smiled at Sacha disarmingly. And she watched him, and thought how polite he always was; in a way, his manners were extremely good.

'Sit down. I will do everything. You are my guest, remember?'

'I don't have a chance to forget, do I?' she answered sweetly. So he felt safer when she wasn't quiet. It would be less of a strain for her too. Being nice to him was difficult, now more so after the visit to the cottage, for she now had the uneasy feeling that he was laughing at her, and that didn't help. Well-mannered indeed, he was an arrogant devil!

49

She sat down at the table and watched him. Before he even touched any food, he washed his hands at the sink, then brought out Sacha's ham and bread.

'I will make tea for us—or do you want wine?' His eyebrow was lifted enquiringly.

She needed her wits about her, and wine always had a soporific effect, but if he drank some . . . 'Just a drop, please.' She had no need to drink more than half a glass, and something told her that if she refused, he wouldn't have any either. He brought a bottle out from the stone pantry, and two tumblers. It was a coarse sharp red wine, the kind that was cheap and plentiful throughout France, and quite delicious with most food.

He filled two glasses and put one in front of Sacha. Then he raised his own. 'Your health,' he said, and drank the wine in one long swallow. She took a deep, very *quiet* breath, and had a cautious sip. Better and better. A couple more glasses and he might be past caring where or when she went.

She buttered the bread as he broke eggs into a basin and heated the black iron pan with a knob of butter in it. When his back was turned, she said, very casually: 'A drop more wine for you?'

'Please,' and he didn't turn round. It took Sacha only a moment to pour half of her own wine into his glass and then top it up from the bottle. And he noticed nothing. Her heart was beating fast, and her mouth was dry, but she had done it.

They ate a few minutes later, and Sacha almost wished she had accepted Tor's offer of an omelette. It was light and fluffy, and he had thrown in a sprinkling of chopped herbs, so that the faint aroma was tantalising and delicious. He finished his second glass of wine and lifted the bottle. 'Some more for you?' he queried.

'No, thanks,' and she blinked. 'Wine makes me sleepy,' she confessed.

He glanced at the nearly empty glass. 'Yes? That is good—you will sleep well,' and then, almost casually, he dropped the bombshell. 'I am afraid that I shall have to stay with you.'

She looked at him, not understanding. 'Stay where?'

He gave an apologetic shrug. 'Tonight. In your room.'

'What!' Her chair went back with a clatter and landed on the floor. Sacha felt the colour drain from her face as she stood looking at him, and for an absurd moment she thought she had drunk too much wine. But she hadn't . . .

She fought for calm. 'I don't understand,' she managed eventually.

'I think you do.' He tapped her nearly empty glass. 'It was very kind of you to give me your wine, but why did you do it? You had only to say no when I asked you.'

She was still too shocked to wonder how he knew. She looked at her bag on the cupboard top.

Could she just make a run for it? A chance might come, but it wasn't now, not yet. She shook her head helplessly, and they faced each other across the table in that long narrow kitchen, and the air bristled with an indefinable tension that was near explosion point. Sacha passed her tongue over dry lips and looked longingly at the wine glinting ruby red lights from the lamp overhead. But she would not touch it now.

'Are you seriously expecting me to sleep in the s-same room with you?' she whispered. 'After what happened——' she pointed her arm, and it was vaguely in the direction of Madame Cassel's, 'there? You must be joking!'

'I know. I am sorry,' but he didn't look it, and Sacha moved angrily away from the table, too tense to stand still a moment longer. She picked up her bag and crossed the living room, opened the front door and stood there. Freedom—so near, and yet so impossibly far . . . so near . . .

'You know you cannot leave.' He was behind her, near her, not touching her, but just standing there. And it was almost as if he *was* touching her, so tense was she.

'I refuse to—to stay with you.' She said it very slowly and clearly, as if it was important for him to understand.

'You do not have a choice.' And what had changed in his tone? It was harder, with a thread of steel running through it, and she turned to look at him. It was there all right, that strength. She had sensed it all along, but now it was unnerving because the gloves were off, and the veneer of gentle humour that she so hated had vanished, and she saw him as he really was. And she stood very still and looked at him, even though she did not want to. She would have preferred to look *anywhere* but at him, but it was like a magnet, his face, shadowed with the light behind him, so that his eyes were too dark to see, but the hard planes, and the strength, were there, and she knew at that moment that this was no ordinary man. His power was real and terrible, and what he said was true; she had no choice.

Suddenly she was trembling, and the more she tried to hide it, the worse it became. She saw him reach into a back pocket, and saw what he brought out; a knife in a sheath. Sacha wanted to move away, but she couldn't. She could only watch in horrified fascination as he slid the cold steel blade from the leather holder, and held it up to the light. Then he said softly: 'This is for you, Sacha.'

CHAPTER THREE

SACHA's legs had turned to jelly, but she gripped
her bag more tightly, ready to jerk it upwards if he
used that knife ... And he put it back in the
leather holder, and handed it to her by holding the
point and resting the handle on the back of his
hand.

'Take it,' he said simply.

'I—I——' Then he saw her face, saw the expression of utter horror, and his eyes narrowed dan-
gerously.

'Did you think I was going to use it on you?' he
asked.

Sacha shook her head. She couldn't speak yet, the
shock had been too great. Tor took her hand,
opened it and put the knife on her palm, then
closed her fingers over it. 'For you,' he said, 'to defend your honour if I try to ravish you.' And the
merest glimmer of a smile accompanied the words.
Sacha found her voice.

'You mean—oh!' She took a deep breath and
looked at the knife. It was long and very slightly
curved and she drew it slowly from the leather
sheath, and the blade glinted whitely and wickedly
in the light. Honed to razor-sharpness, it was frightening. She slid it back with a shudder.

'How do you know I won't s-stab you with it so that I can get away?' she asked.

'You will not. I *know*.' His dark eyes met and held hers unblinkingly. 'You could not knife me in "cold blood"—that is the expression, yes? But I think, to defend yourself, if you *had* to, you would. And so'—he shrugged in that graceful, eloquent way he had—'do you think I would try anything? No. You are safe with me—and I think you will feel safer with that, will you not?'

She knew what he meant—she knew *exactly*—and what he said was true. Yet how did he understand her so well? That was something she could not fathom.

She put her hand up to her eyes, lest he see the quick tears of tiredness well up. What was the use? He wasn't going to let her get away, she realised that now. And she wondered what would have happened if Nigel had come with her. How would he have coped? But that was something too difficult to contemplate. And her father? What of him? Sacha usually phoned or wrote on arrival, but he wouldn't worry, not for a couple of days, for when he was immersed in his painting, the passage of time became irrelevant, and in two or three days, he might—but by then she should be free—*should be* . . .

'Go upstairs,' he said quietly. 'Go now. I will follow soon.' He stood quite still as she went across the living room to the stairs without looking back, so that she did not see the expression on his face, nor the muscle that tightened in his dark jaw.

She lay in bed, on her back, the knife under her pillow. She had slipped off her sandals after washing, and lay fully clothed with only one lavender-scented sheet on her. The rain pattered on the open window, and a faint cool draught came from it as the door was opened softly. She stiffened and closed her eyes, and with her right hand felt for the reassuring weapon beneath her head. Half an hour had passed since she had come up, and the house might have been empty. She had crept along the landing after washing and stood very still outside the door under which a thin strip of yellow showed. There had been voices, and faint music—and the occasional click-click—as if they were playing chess. Perhaps they were. The Russians were great chess players, and it was one way of whiling away the time while they were waiting. But for what? Sacha didn't know, and after a few moments she had crept along to the bedroom she was to occupy, well aware that it would be useless to creep down and try to get out, for she had heard Tor lock the doors after she had left him, and the bolts were old and stiff, and creaked . . .

He stood quite still and she knew he was looking down at her. She kept her breathing deep and even, and perhaps she fooled him, for a moment later she felt his hands on the bed . . . Then he pulled a thin blanket over her, very carefully and slowly, and made no attempt to touch her ... She heard the sound of his espadrilles and the other bed creaked, and he was lying down. Sacha kept her eyes closed, and listened to the rain outside to try and calm herself. She was afraid because of the very strangeness of the situation. A man she had never even known existed seven hours previously was lying in bed only feet away from her, a stranger, Russian and very tough, with a fiery temper. She had seen it for a few moments when she had made her first abortive escape attempt, and been very frightened by it.

And now she tried to think, but it was difficult. The strain of what had happened was making her extremely tired. She was trying to stay awake, but her eyes were heavy, and the small amount of wine she had drunk was having an effect, even if only slight, and now it was easier to keep her eyes closed instead of opening them, and her hand was on the knife, ready for if she should hear him get out of bed, and she would think in a minute, she would...

When she opened her eyes the rain had stopped, and the moon shed a ghostly sheen over everything in the room. Sacha looked round, saw the sleeping man so near that she could lean and touch him— and she remembered where she was, and who *he* was, and she sat up. She was drenched in perspiration, and the memory of a bad dream was still strong so that she reached up to touch her cheek, because in the dream someone had been threatening her with a knife . . . And she remembered the one she had been given by Tor, and felt underneath her pillow, and it was there.

She looked over at the man lying on his side, with his back to her. His breathing was deep and even, and he lay at an angle, one arm beneath his head, the other, his left, hanging down almost over the edge of the bed. He had taken his shirt off, and lay with only a blanket to cover him. The moonlight gleamed on his skin, turning it pale silver—and she saw the darkening bruise on his shoulder as she quietly slipped out of bed, and crept barefoot to the door. Very, *very* quietly, so as not to . . .

'Where are you going?' His accent was strong, perhaps because he was half asleep still, and Sacha froze in her tracks.

'To—to the bathroom,' she answered, and wondered if he could hear her heart hammering against her ribs.

He sat up, and she turned round to see him. Then go. And remember—I have locked the doors downstairs. If you try to open one, I shall hear—and you will not get away.'

'I wouldn't try.' She slipped out, wishing she had the knife with her.

When she went back he was lying down again. She went over to the window to look out, and to feel the soft rain-washed night air on her face. It was probably three o'clock in the morning, and away in the big resorts, Nice, Cannes and others, people would still be up, drinking and dancing the night away. Even as she stood there she seemed to hear faint music borne on the still air, and it was probably only her imagination, but it made her feel very lost and alone. She gripped the windowsill tightly and looked down. So near, the ground, dark and welcoming. Oh, for a rope!

She heard the Russian stir, as if impatient to go back to sleep, but she stayed where she was. Let him wait.

'Sacha,' he said. She didn't answer.

He repeated it and she looked round slowly. 'Well? What do you want?' She mentally measured the distance to her bed. Let him try anything . . .

'Can you not sleep?'

'No.' It was true now. She had had her first deep vital sleep, and she was wide awake. 'I want to go out for a walk,' she said. What would he think of *that* idea! Perversely she wanted to annoy him. If she succeeded, he didn't show it. He merely laughed and said:

'Get back in your bed.'

'No. I like standing here.'

'Do you? Then shall I come and stand with you —and we will watch the moon together, yes? That would be nice, I think.' And she heard the slither of a sheet and turned hurriedly, because that was the last thing she wanted—and he laughed, as if he *knew*—and Sacha's anger, the hopeless, *helpless*

59

anger of being frustrated by this *powerful*, unpredictable man, all the time, spilt over and she launched herself at him, pummelling at him with her fists, and if she had stopped to think about it she would have realised how foolish it was, in more ways than one, but she didn't—it was an impulsive action doomed from the start. And yet she had to try.

It was as if he were ready for her—he was always ready for anything she might do—she should have known that.

He pulled her down on top of him, just as simply as that. Only then she wasn't on top of him, she was underneath, imprisoned by his hard body and legs, and he was holding her hands so that she was as completely helpless as a fly caught in a web.

'Now,' he said, and he wasn't laughing any more, 'how do you like that, eh, Miss Sacha?'

She lay very still, and most strangely, it wasn't unpleasant being there. He wasn't hurting her. But she was thinking all the time. Thinking hard, wondering what on earth she was going to do next —and where, oh, where was the knife?

'You see,' he went on without waiting for the answer that he knew she didn't intend to give, 'I have a black belt in judo and karate. And do you really think, even if I had not, that you, a girl, could hope to fight me?'

Sacha was silent. No use to argue, to say anything at all. She twisted her head sideways and waited for him to release her. And waited ... and felt him move, and his hand came up to touch her face as he whispered: 'Very nice, *very* nice, Miss Sacha Donnelly, and now I think——' and he kissed her, and it was a very gentle kiss, but his lips weren't soft, they were hard and warm, and her lips burned like fire.

She was frightened. 'Oh no—please——' she said. Tor pulled her up and knelt in front of her on the bed. His breathing was heavy and his voice harsh as he said:

'Then do not tempt fate, little one. Do you not know what you are doing, or are you so innocent that you do not understand the ways of men? Tell me.'

He suddenly kicked the sheet off and stood up, pulling Sacha up after him, yet keeping hold of her hand. 'I am waiting for an answer,' he said softly. He wore only his shorts, and out of the corner of her eye she saw the glint of her keys and some others, and a wallet, on the chair at the side of the bed. But she couldn't think about those now. He was waiting for her to speak.

As he held her hand, he was rubbing his thumb along her wrist, lightly massaging it, and it was curiously soothing. 'I don't know what you mean,' she said carefully. 'You think that because I'm here —your "guest" as you call it, but I'm a prisoner, aren't I?—that you can do anything you like. I hate you.' Her voice shook as she said the last three words.

'No, you do not. You don't know me well enough to hate me. Dislike me, yes, perhaps—because of what I have done. But hate is a very bad word. I am sure you do not hate anybody.'

She looked into his face, silvery grey, shadowed in the cool light of the moon. 'You don't know me at all,' she said.

'I know you very well. And you have not answered my question. Do you not know what is likely to happen when you throw yourself on a man who is in bed? Tell me. Because if you do not, perhaps you should learn before you get yourself into a difficult situation, no?'

She pulled her hand away from that disturbingly familiar caress.

'I don't need you to teach me,' she retorted.

The faint gleam of white showed as he smiled. 'No?' he shrugged. 'A pity. Still—I gave you my word—and you have the knife.' He gave a mock shudder. 'I nearly forgot that. I would be very foolish to tangle with you, little English miss, would I not?'

He was mocking her, but it wasn't cruel, she sensed that. She turned away and went over to her bed.

'I thought you wanted to go out for a walk,' he said.

She breathed in sharply. 'Yes, but——'

62

'Then we will go. Come. I shall not sleep either any more. Then we will drink some wine, or coffee —whichever *you* prefer—and come back to bed.' He makes it sound so cosy, she thought bitterly. As if she *were* on holiday! But a tingle of excitement stirred inside her. A walk, in the moonlight, at three o'clock in the morning. She had never done that before. And even if she didn't like him, it wouldn't matter for half an hour, and she certainly wouldn't sleep now—not after *that* little incident —she felt herself go warm at the memory, and turned quickly away in case anything showed in her face.

'All right. I'll get another sweater to pull on over this.' She bent to her suitcase, and he went over to the door and switched the light on, flooding the room with brilliance so that she blinked at the suddenness of it.

She pulled out a long-line cardigan. It was white, but it would do—she hadn't the strength to try and run away at the moment . . .

'Right?' He had his shirt on, and his espadrilles —and she looked at him.

'Won't you be cold?'

'I have my sweater downstairs. Let us go.' Then he clicked his fingers. 'Ah, the knife. Where did you put it?'

'Under my pillow—but why?——' she watched him lean over and pick it up, and something, the faintest thread of fear and suspicion, touched the back of her neck. 'Why are you taking it?' she asked quietly.

'Why? Because——' he shrugged. 'Because night time can be dangerous. Come.'

She followed him down the stairs, and at the bottom he turned and put his finger to his lips. 'I will get my sweater from the kitchen. Wait here, please.' And she watched him lope off silently.

A few minutes later they were walking down the stony track towards the main road. He had locked the door behind him, with the big old key, and slipped it into his pocket.

When they reached the fateful spot of their first shattering encounter, Sacha stopped. 'Where is my car?' she asked him.

'Behind the house, in the garage. It is safe.'

'My painting things are in it.'

'I know. You shall have them tomorrow. You may paint if you wish.'

'Where?' she asked dryly. 'Down on the beach?'

He appraised her smilingly. 'In the garden— where I can see you.'

'Yes, I thought so.' Something had changed. She couldn't put her finger on it, but something— *about him*—was different. She didn't know what it was, but it wasn't frightening. On the contrary, it was almost a relaxing of tension between them. And she was to know, soon enough—she would guess.

The path was very stony, and it was difficult to

see all the tiny rocks and pebbles, for moonlight was deceptive and threw false shadows. But he walked as sure-footed as a cat, and Sacha recalled what he had told her about his being a black belt in judo and karate. She believed him. She believed the other things he had said too—and that he would never consciously or deliberately hurt her physically; whatever he was, however bad, she sensed in him the instincts of chivalry, not to hurt or mistreat a woman. It was reassuring in one way. But there were so many other things that were frightening, and these he would not, or could not, explain.

Once, when she stumbled, she instinctively clutched at his arm to stop herself falling. His left arm. She felt rather than heard him wince, and she remembered that dark bruise, and bit her lip.

'Have you a first aid box at the house?' she asked him.

'Yes. Why?' he turned a puzzled face towards her.

'I'll bandage your shoulder,' she said.

'Pooh!' he laughed, and put his arm round her waist. 'See, it is strong enough to take care of a pretty girl.' She didn't mind him doing it any more, but she didn't want *him* to know that, so she stiffened slightly for a moment.

It was truly beautiful to be out at that time of the night—or morning—Sacha wasn't sure which. The clouds had all gone, and the stars were out in that velvety darkness, and the white ghostly moon floated very high and remote, and she looked up at it, and stopped walking. 'Oh, look!' she exclaimed. 'Look at it. I thought it would be different, once men had walked there—but it's not. It's just the same as ever.'

He looked down at her, and smiled, but didn't say anything. And they stood still for several minutes on that dusty rough track with the weeds poking through in places, and high walls on either side, and Sacha suddenly went cold.

'I want to go back,' she whispered.

'Why? What is it?' he asked, his voice sharp.

She looked at him. 'Nothing. It's just——' but she couldn't explain what she did mean, only that she was aware of a waiting stillness in the air—as if something or someone was watching them. The impression had been fleeting, merely an instant, but something lingered so that she added: 'I'm afraid.'

'Of me?' he queried, and smiled.

'No—of something. Or someone. I feel as if I'm being watched.' She saw the smile leave his face suddenly. Then he did a strange thing. He put his arm round her, and hugging her, said something in Russian—and before she could ask him what he thought he was doing, he kissed her soundly. At the end, he whispered in her ear:

'Act normally, keep your arm round me, and we

66

will walk slowly back. You understand me?'

'Y-yes.'

He squeezed her arm. 'Good. Come.'

Together they walked back, and once or twice he laughed, as if they had been whispering and she had said something funny. But she was cold inside, for she knew now what the difference in him was, and why he had agreed to go for a walk, and she loathed him.

Inside the house she waited until he had bolted the door and turned towards her, then she brought her hand up and struck him across his face with all her strength.

There was a tense silence for a moment. Then he spoke, furious, she could tell. 'Why did you do that?'

'You *know*. Because you used me just then—took me out for a purpose——' she watched the mark of her fingers grow from white to red on his face, but he made no move to touch his cheek, merely looked at her, his eyes dark and dangerous.

'And if I did?'

'I don't like it. I know you're up to no good—and perhaps whoever is watching us and this house isn't any good either, but I don't want to be used. Did you imagine they think I am your "wife"—the one you're supposed to be on honeymoon with?' Her mouth trembled with the effort to speak.

He shrugged. 'Perhaps—and perhaps you imagined someone watching. You women see things where there are only shadows, and hear noises—'

'Then you must do too!' she shot back angrily. 'For I saw your face change. And that's why you took the knife—' she put her hand to her mouth, feeling sick. He took the holstered knife from his pocket and held it out to her.

'Take it.'

For answer she knocked it out of his hand and it skidded several feet across the floor. 'Keep it. I'm sure you're better at using one than me—ouch! let go of my arm!'

Tor had a grip of steel, and he was angry. 'Sometimes,' he grated, 'sometimes it would be much easier if you were not a woman—'

'Oh yes, wouldn't it! Let me *go*! You're so much stronger than everyone else, aren't you?' Then as he released her wrist, she rubbed it and looked at him accusingly.

'You said—you had to know a person before you could hate them. Well, I know you now—and I hate *you*!' And she turned and ran up the stairs without once looking back.

He didn't go to bed at all again that night. Sacha lay awake for ages before falling asleep, and when at last she woke, the bright sunlight streamed through the window and Tor's bed was just as he had left it before their fateful walk. For one dreadful moment she wondered if something had happened to him, then she sank back on her pillow. Of course not! She could smell food cooking, spicy herby smells, and the tang of freshly ground coffee.

The painful incident of the night might never have happened. Her door was ajar, and somewhere on the landing a board creaked, and outside a gull shrieked as if in derision. Sacha struggled into a sitting position and rubbed her eyes. She was hungry. That was the one thing she was sure of. But she couldn't just go down, like that. For memory was flooding back, and it was painful to remember what had actually happened—and what she had said—and worse, done . . .

She hunched up and clasped her hands over her knees, and thought back—then a tap came on the door, then Tor's voice: 'May I come in?'

Sacha looked at the door, waited, swallowed, then said quietly: 'Yes.'

He carried a steaming beaker. His voice was cool and distant as he said: 'Good morning. I have brought you coffee. You wish for breakfast up here?'

'No. I'll come down if—if I may.'

'Yes. But not for a few minutes. Drink that first, then wash. Then you may come down.'

'All right.' She watched him pull up the chair near the bed, and put the coffee on it. The keys and wallet had gone—so he had been up before, but she hadn't heard him. She looked round her in quiet despair. It was Friday, and her holiday was just beginning; the weather was perfect, everything should have been pleasant and ordered, and she would have been going to visit Tante Marie today, and perhaps do a little painting in the garden later on—but what would happen now? Sacha began to sip the hot sweet coffee. It was good and strong, and from somewhere Tor had bought milk—perhaps from a nearby farm—and he had made it just right, just as she liked it. But she wouldn't tell him.

An idea, born of her determination, began to form in her mind as she finished the drink. She took a deep breath. It was worth trying. She had nothing to lose—only that he might refuse, and she half expected that anyway. And so, when she was at the breakfast table, she said: 'I have promised to visit my aunt today. She is expecting me—and she is very old—I don't want to worry her by n-not going,' she nearly faltered at the sight of his face. And then he took her breath away completely.

'All right. You can go—with me.' They were both eating. Sacha had insisted on making her own omelette—perhaps in a kind of way, trying to show him—but exactly what, she wasn't sure.

She looked up, stunned, and he raised his coffee cup in a half mocking gesture before drinking it.

'Did you think I would refuse?'

'Yes,' she admitted.

'Well, I did not. And do you know why? Because this time I believe you. You were lying about your father coming—you do not tell good lies, Sacha— but I think what you say now is true.' He gave a dry humourless smile. 'And we will soon see, eh?'

She looked quickly down at her plate to hide a flare of triumph from his keen eyes. Her quick brain raced ahead checking possibilities . . .

'But I warn you now not to try anything at all. I shall watch you closely—'

She tried to laugh. 'Heavens! Of course not. Tante Marie is very old. Anything like—that—would kill her—I wouldn't dream—' she stopped, in case she was protesting too much. Tante Marie might be old, but she was far from frail—even if she *looked* it—and that was what mattered.

'May I ask how you come to have a French aunt?'

She was willing to be civil to him now, and he had lost some of his previous air of cool formality. 'Well, she's not exactly an aunt, but my father had some very good friends in France during the war—he was over here on secret work—and Tante Marie is the mother of one of them. This man died soon afterwards, but my father has always kept in touch with the old lady, and we always visit her. She is over eighty.' And a sudden thought assailed her, almost frightening. 'You won't—I mean—' she faltered at the hard greyness of his eyes as they met hers.

'Yes?' You are perhaps thinking that I will kidnap her?' A slight smile touched the corner of his mouth. 'I do not think there is room here, do you? And remember—it is up to you to behave yourself.

71

Do you understand the meaning of my words?'

She understood all right. Only too well. 'Yes, I do,' she answered slowly.

'Good.' He stood and took his plate to the sink. 'You are beginning to learn some sense—perhaps you are even beginning to believe that I spoke the truth when I said I meant you no harm?'

But Sacha wasn't going to answer that. She carried her plate to the sink after him, and said: 'I'll wash up.'

'As you wish. Thank you.' And he walked out and left her alone. She glared at his retreating back, and she could not have said how she felt at that moment. A turmoil of mixed emotions, she felt hopelessly confused inside. But above all, she thought she would never understand the man called Tor.

She changed into a cool white sleeveless shift dress and sandals, washed her previous day's clothes and hung them out to dry on the line at the back of the house. It was a baking hot day, the sun boring relentlessly down from a bright blue sky, and the clothes would be dry in less than an hour, she knew. A plane droned distantly, and she breathed deeply of the eucalyptus-scented air, hearing the unmistakable chirrup of the cicadas that lived in the trees and kept up a constant cheek-cheek from morning to night. After a while you stopped hearing it, but it was still new enough for Sacha to enjoy. She stood still for a few moments, wondering if Tor would let her drive the Citroën, or insist himself. She was in for a shock.

They set off after a very early lunch. Tor seemed to have spent a lot of time with the other two men, talking quietly in their room while she waited outside where he could see her.

He ran down the stairs and came to the front door. He had changed—very much so—and yet they were only simple differences—but he could easily have been another man. Sacha stood looking at him, startled, and he grinned.

'It is me. Yes, really,' he said.

'Do you always disguise yourself when you go out?' she asked dryly.

'Disguise?' He took off the sunglasses and whipped off the battered straw hat, virtually part of the Riviera 'uniform' that he had been wearing. 'You call this a disguise?'

They did make a difference, though. He wore faded blue denims, and a white shirt instead of his previous day's outfit. The same espadrilles, and Sacha saw the faint bulge of the knife in his back pocket and her mouth tightened. But she dared not say anything for fear he would refuse to go.

He put the sunglasses back on, and they were almost sinister—and yet very attractive. He tilted the battered straw hat forward lazily and reached out to take Sacha's arm. 'Come,' he said. They walked round the back of the house and she waited confidently for him to go over to the Citroën—and saw him instead go to his motorbike.

Her heart sank. 'Oh no—please——' she began. He looked round, half astride, and frowned.

'What is the matter now?'

'I rather thought we would be going in the car,' she faltered.

'This is better—is quicker. See. Get on behind me and put your arms round me.'

Biting her lip, Sacha did so and sat gingerly on the pillion seat. He half turned his head. 'I said put your arms round me. If you don't you will fall off.'

She gritted her teeth—but if she wanted to go she would have to do as he said.

'I've never been on one of these before,' she had to admit.

'No?' He laughed. 'Then it is an experience you will not forget. Are you ready?'

'Yes,' her voice was muffled, because in putting her arms round him she had to lean forward as well, and her face was half buried somewhere between his broad shoulders. His body was warm and hard, with not a spare ounce of fat. All muscle and bone, and she found to her horror that she was actually enjoying holding him, and it made her shift guiltily, uneasily. He didn't appear to notice.

'Hold tight, Sacha. We go now.'

He kicked the starter and revved up, and she closed her eyes, terrified, and waited for what was to happen. It was worse than she could have imagined. As they shot off down the path from the house to the track she held on grimly, feeling as if she was about to fall off any second. For one dreadful moment it had been like being poised at the topmost part of the scenic railway at a fair before that breathless, *screaming* plunge down, faster and faster ... And then they were on the track itself, and that was worse, because it was so bumpy, and he had to keep making little swerving movements to dodge the rocks and potholes.

Clinging tighter than she had ever clung to anybody, Sacha buried her face in Tor's back and waited for the crash.

Then suddenly and miraculously he was slowing down, and she ventured to open one eye. Surely they weren't in Cannes already?

'Sacha, you are liking it? You are holding me tight, yes?'

'I'm praying,' she answered, and she wasn't really joking at all, but he laughed. They had stopped simply because they had reached the end of the track, where it widened into the main road, and he was waiting for a gap in the traffic.

He turned to her. 'Are you truly frightened?'

She didn't see any point in pretending. 'Yes.'

He switched off the engine. 'I am sorry. Do you wish to go back and we will take the car?'

She thought for a moment that he must be joking, and looked quickly at him. But his face was

75

perfectly serious, and he was waiting for her answer. She shook her head slowly. 'No. It's all right —I'll be okay in a minute. I just didn't know what it was like.'

'I promise you we are over the worst. See——' he pointed back up the track. 'That was bad for us. Now is smooth. And I will not go too fast.'

She swallowed. 'Yes. I'm being silly, please go on.'

He kicked it into life again, and she felt the throb of the engine beneath her, the surge of power waiting to thrust them forward. And now, strangely enough, because she had told him of her fear, she was no longer frightened. She held on again, but not so desperately, and he saw a gap in the constant stream of cars, and wove into it.

It was better. He had spoken the truth. And after a few miles of superbly smooth riding, gently weaving in and out, not going too fast, she began to enjoy herself, began to understand the keen pleasure that can come from being on such a comparatively fragile machine as opposed to a safer car.

Tor must have sensed this, for he called back: 'Now, is better, eh?' Sacha heard the words before the wind snatched them away, and shouted:

'Yes, it's wonderful!'

They had to stop for petrol on the outskirts of Cannes. Opposite the garage was a café, with tables and brightly coloured umbrellas on the pavement, and a small walled garden at the back. Sacha was standing waiting, Tor close by her side, and her legs were trembling with the strain of holding on. Tor looked at her.

'Do you want a drink?'

She looked at him quickly. 'Can we? I mean——' she bit her lip.

He grinned, very tanned and handsome behind those mysterious glasses. 'Just as long as you behave —do you understand me?'

'Oh yes,' she breathed. She was so thirsty, she would have promised anything, and she was too weak to run—although *he* didn't know that.

'Come, then. You will give me your aunt's address while we are sitting down.'

He paid for the petrol and left the bike to one side of the garage. He took her arm protectively as they crossed the road, and she felt very small beside him.

'Here, in the garden. It is nicer, I think,' he told her, and opened the green gate.

'And no people,' she murmured, but he heard, and laughed.

'That is better! You are getting some of your spirit back. You know, Sacha,' and he pulled one of the white wrought-iron chairs out for her in a corner of the garden, 'I was getting worried about you. I thought you had lost some of the fire.'

'Did you?' She looked round, because for some reason she wanted to fix this in her memory—but she didn't know why. The wall behind them was of rough grey stone, and little blue flowers grew in the crevices. A huge copper tub stood on the ground beside them, with a feathery palm flourishing inside, and yellow flowers growing beside it. There was a smell of petrol and garlic in the air, and faint perfume, but she couldn't recognise it, and that was annoying.

'M'sieur?' The blue-jowled Italian waiter was polite, but in a hurry to get back to a delectable blonde who sat alone on a pavement chair. Tor cocked an eyebrow at Sacha.

'What will you have?'

'Something long and cold, please.'

'Deux menthes avec limonade, s'il vous plaît.'

She pulled a face, and Tor frowned. 'Wait until you taste it before you do that.'

'All right.' He pulled out his cigarettes and offered Sacha one, but she refused. She watched him light his and put his lighter down by the shell ashtray on the red-topped table. He sat back negligently and tipped the hat forward on his head. She couldn't see his eyes because of the glasses, but she knew that he was watching her and it made her vaguely uneasy. She looked round, but they were the only occupants of the garden, unless you counted the black cat sitting on the wall watching a fly.

Sacha opened her bag to find her mirror because she felt as if she must have chewed all her lipstick off at the beginning of the journey—and she knew that something was missing. Frowning, she riffled through the contents again, and he said softly: 'What is it?'

Then she knew what had gone, and caught her breath. 'My passport. It's not here,' she said, and looked across the table at him. 'Have you taken it?'

'Me?' he seemed almost amused. 'Why should I?'

'Do you have to hide behind those glasses?' she demanded. 'I can't see you.'

He took them off slowly. 'Is that better?' He put them on the table, and every movement was deliberate. 'You will perhaps find your passport when you return to the house——'

'I might—but it didn't drop out of my bag, if that's what you're going to say next——' She had to stop to allow the waiter to put two long glasses full of sparkling dark green liquid with pieces of orange and lemon floating in it on the table. 'Because the catch is a good one, and I never leave it unfastened,' she continued when he had gone. 'And you were in my room when I was asleep—before you brought in my coffee—because your keys and wallet had gone from the chair.'

'Ah,' he nodded. 'You think well. That is good.'

'*Did* you?' she demanded, too worried to drink. 'Did I what?'

'Take my passport.' Helpless anger filled her. She had never met a man who could so fill her with impotent rage. Whatever happened, it was as if he had the upper hand all the time.

He nodded. 'Yes. But it is safe—and it will be

returned to you. We want it only for a little while.'

'Why?' her eyes were wide, and she knew the colour had drained from her face.

'To see if you are who you say you are,' he explained.

'But how—' she had to stop and take a swallow of the icy green minty drink, and was too agitated to notice just how delicious it was. 'How c-can you?'

'There are ways.'

'I am Sacha Donnelly,' she insisted. 'Look.' With a sudden desperate movement she took the locket from her neck, the one she wore always, because her mother had given it to her five years previously, just before she died. 'Open it. Read what it says. My mother gave me that, and it is very precious to me.'

He took the fragile gold chain in his fingers, and she held her breath, fearing that it would snap, but his hands were careful as he opened it and looked at the tiny oval picture of Mrs. Donnelly, and the delicately carved inscription in the lid: 'Sacha, from Mummy.' And the date.

She gave him time to read it, then reached out for it back.

'Please,' she said. She regretted her impulsive action, but it was too late. 'Do you think I forged *that*?' she breathed. 'Do you?' And tears glistened brightly in her eyes, but stayed unshed. And if he answered 'yes', she didn't know what she would do.

'No,' he answered slowly. 'That is real.'

Sacha bent her head to put the chain on, and looked down into the glass. A lemon pip floated slowly to the sparkling green surface and she blinked quickly several times. Her fingers stupidly refused to fasten the catch, and she caught her breath. Then Tor moved behind her, smoothing the silky soft hair from her neck as he said: 'Permit me.' The back of her head tingled at his gentle touch and she sat very still as he went on: 'But it is necessary to *know*. It is very important.' It was done and he moved back to his seat; the memory of his touch lingered so that Sacha would not look at him as she said:

'I don't see why.'

'You will, soon. Now give me your aunt's address, please, and then we will go.'

'It's fourteen Rue Tissot. It's a big block of flats.'

'I know them,' he answered surprisingly.

'I won't be a minute.' She picked up her glass.

'There is no hurry.' He turned and beckoned the waiter. 'Do you wish for another drink?'

'No, thanks, but don't let me stop you.'

He shrugged. 'It does not matter.' She watched him pay the bill, add a tip, and the waiter spared them a brief flash of his teeth before walking away. Sacha bit her lip. Clever Tor! The tip had been just right. Not too much so that he would be remembered, not too little so that again he would be easily recalled, for another reason—but just enough.

She finished her drink and stood up. Tor followed her out, sunglasses firmly on again, and took her arm as before when they crossed the road.

'I'm not going to run,' she said bitterly. 'I know better than to try—with you.'

He smiled. 'Good. That makes it easier for me.'

He was never lost for an answer, never remotely embarrassed at anything she said. She was wasting her breath, she knew, in trying to upset him.

He waited until she was holding him firmly before he kicked the motorbike into life, and drove away from the front and the sea to the higher, quieter part of Cannes. They would soon be there, and Sacha felt a tingle of anticipation. What would happen?

CHAPTER FOUR

SACHA soon found out. Tor was utterly and absolutely charming to the old lady who sat waiting for them on the balcony of her flat. She stood and watched him as she introduced him. It didn't seem possible that this was the same man that *she* knew. Just as effectively as the slight change in dress had altered him, so was his manner changed, once he entered the flat.

As they had walked up the two flights of stairs—the lift was once again out of order—he had said: 'I am staying at Madame Cassel's home, and I am alone. Do you understand?'

'Yes,' Sacha had nodded.

'Good. And please do not try anything. Remember I shall be watching you.'

'I've told you—she's an old woman.'

'Yes, I know. Do you speak English or French to her?'

'Both. She likes to practise her English—but when she gets tired, we switch to French.'

He nodded, but said nothing, and she began to wonder if she had made a bad mistake in coming. It had seemed such a good idea when he had first agreed—but she would have to be very careful.

The blank paper and a pencil were in her bag, because she hadn't decided what to write—and it was safer that way at the moment.

For Sacha's main hope was in giving a note to Hortense, Tante Marie's maid, who only went home late every evening—and who knew when to keep her mouth shut . . .

The door was ajar. 'Come in, come in.' Tante Marie was little and plump, and she could walk, but only with difficulty, so that for most of the day she would sit on a white wrought iron chair on the roomy balcony, surrounded by dozens of her beloved potted plants, her 'garden', as she referred to it.

Her hair was always immaculately swept back with tortoise-shell combs, her eyes a pale faded blue now, but keen as a girl's—and Sacha had never seen her dressed in anything else but black satin, with a cameo brooch at the high lace neck of her dress.

A lump came into her throat as she went forward to greet the old lady, and to kneel by the wheelchair she sat in.

'Oh, Tante Marie, it's so wonderful to see you again!'

'And you, *ma petite*, but who have you brought for me? a friend?'

'Oh. Yes. I'd like you to meet——' she hesitated for only a second, 'Tor. He is a guest at Madame Cassel's house. Tor, this is Madame Beauvais.'

He came forward from where he had been waiting, just inside the door. In his left hand the battered straw hat and sunglasses, his right outstretched to take that of the old woman who watched him keenly. He bowed over it, as if it were quite natural to do so, and there was a dignity about him that moved Sacha in a strange way.

'*Enchanté, madame,*' he said. Tante Marie's eyebrows shot up.

'*Tiens!* And where are you from, young man? Eh? Sit down, sit down both of you. You'll give me a stiff neck if I have to keep looking at you up there. That's better!' This with warm approval as Tor lifted forward two heavy dining chairs as if they were made of balsa wood and set them side by side in front of her.

Sacha had the absurd desire to laugh hysterically. *He* had come hoping to question the old lady undoubtedly, while Tante Marie now seemed about to conduct her own inquisition. Sacha had forgotten just how curious she was about everything and everybody. They would be well matched, she thought wryly. Then she sobered. Where was Hortense? A minute later the maid was forgotten as she listened with a kind of growing dismay and astonishment mixed at the conversation between the two.

Tante Marie's face had lit up delightedly. 'Moscow! Ah, yes, that brings back the memories!'

'You have been, *madame*?'

'But yes! Has my Sacha not told you? Tch! I lived there as a child for several years—just outside Leningrad. My father was an engineer at the court of the Tzar——' Sacha watched Tor. Gone the hardness she had so often seen. Gone too that ready smile that meant nothing, she now knew. He was listening quite intently to the old woman, answering her questions, asking his own, patient and polite—and Sacha was forgotten.

At a lull in the conversation, she asked: 'Where is Hortense?'

'What?' They both turned to look at her as if she were a stranger who had suddenly burst in on them.

'Oh, the silly woman has gone to a wedding— some distant niece. She'll be sorry she missed you. Eh, Sacha, go and bring my box of photographs— there, from the corner—yes, yes, there—that one. Ah, that's it.' The old lady settled the large chocolate box on her knee and began to undo the fastening ribbons with slightly trembly fingers.

'If you will permit, *madame*?' As he undid the ribbons, Tante Marie looked up at Sacha and winked. Tor couldn't see, his head was bent, but Sacha knew that wink only too well. She closed her mouth tightly. If only the old woman *knew*! Then her idea came to her. She stood up, very casually, still holding her bag.

'I'll go and make coffee, shall I, Tante? While you're showing Tor your photographs?' And she would have the perfect excuse to be out for several minutes . . .

'*Mais oui, certainement!* You know where everything is. Hortense made a chocolate cake before she went. It is in the blue tin—'

But Sacha, nodding and smiling, and with her bag under her arm, was half way out to the kitchen before she finished speaking. There was a tiny passage; the kitchen led off it, as did bedroom and bathroom and clothes closet. She pushed the door behind her. First step safely over. Who would have dreamed they would get on like that! What a god-send. She put the percolator on the gas, then quickly opened her bag and began to feel for the paper . . .

'And shall I make coffee, or cut the cake?' Sacha spun guiltily round at the lazy voice from the doorway, her bag skidding to the floor. Tor stood there, one arm on the doorpost, the other on his lean hip. Before she could move he bent and scooped the bag up, and her pencil fell out with a tiny clatter to the black-tiled floor.

'Oh, I am so clumsy! The point has broken.' He handed her the bag and pencil. Her heartbeat had steadied.

'I thought you were looking at photos,' she said lightly.

'Not yet. Madame Beauvais is sorting out the ones she wishes to show me. I offered to help you. Do not worry, I have put the small table by her and she is quite happy looking through the box for a few minutes.' Then he added softly: 'Did you think I would let you out of my sight?'

'I don't really know. Does it matter? If you want to help, the cake tin is the one on top of the cupboard. Plates on a shelf inside.' She turned away, feigning indifference. He could hardly follow her to the bathroom if she went. She bit back a giggle at the thought.

Tante Marie was proudly trying out her meagre Russian, and if Tor winced inwardly, he was careful not to show it. They had drunk coffee and eaten the most delicious chocolate cake in the world, and the conversation had never once faltered, and Sacha became a willing listener because somehow, and much to her own surprise, she was finding out that the details of Tor's life years ago were utterly fascinating. She could almost see him going to school, walking down ice-hard roads in winter, muffled up to the eyes because it was below freezing and there was no transport between the farm where he lived and the school. Whatever he had become now, however bad, she knew he was speaking the truth, and that in a way he too was going back in time, seeing everything anew because of an old lady, who couldn't bear not to know everything about everyone.

Now they were talking in that most unfamiliar language, and Sacha listened, absorbed, and watched him. She didn't *want* to watch him—all

From Harlequin...a special offer for women who enjoy reading fascinating stories of great romance in exciting places...

ACCEPT THIS "COLLECTOR'S EDITION" FREE...

...JUST FOR TELLING US WHY YOU LIKE TO READ ROMANTIC FICTION!

Please take a minute to fill out the attached questionnaire... affix your "YES" stamp... and mail today! We pay postage.

Harlequin's Collection 1

VIOLET WINSPEAR
Lucifer's Angel

Keep your free copy of this special "Collector's Edition"...

Please answer the simple questions on the card, detach and mail today. We'll be happy to send you this special "Collector's Edition" of *Lucifer's Angel* by Violet Winspear absolutely free. It's our way of saying "Thank you" for helping us publish more of the kind of books you like to read.

LUCIFER'S ANGEL

One of the classic romance novels by this world-renowned author!
You'll enjoy reading Violet Winspear's explosive story of the fast-moving hard-living world of Hollywood in the '50s. It's an unforgettable tale of an innocent young girl who meets and marries a dynamic but ruthless movie producer. It's a gripping novel combining excitement, intrigue, mystery and romance.

Newly printed in a special "Collector's Edition"! We've published a brand new "Collector's Edition" of Violet Winspear's first Harlequin novel. And a complimentary copy is waiting for you. Just fill out the card and mail today.

FREE BOOK

DETACH STAMP, MOISTEN AND AFFIX BELOW BEFORE MAILING!

TO GET YOUR FREE COPY OF "LUCIFER'S ANGEL" ... PLEASE TELL US WHAT YOU THINK ABOUT ROMANCE NOVELS.

WHETHER YOU SAY "YES" OR "NO" PLEASE TELL US WHAT YOU THINK ABOUT ROMANCE NOVELS

Moisten
and affix
free book
stamp
here

Just take a minute to answer these brief questions...
1. I regularly read more than 4 Harlequin novels a month
YES ☐ NO ☐. 2. I quite often pass along my Harlequin
books to my friends   YES ☐ NO ☐.   3. I would read more
Harlequin novels if they were more easily available
YES ☐ NO ☐. 4. I especially enjoy reading Harlequin
books because: I like good readable stories YES ☐ NO ☐.
The characters are fascinating YES ☐ NO ☐. I enjoy reading about far-away places YES ☐ NO ☐. The
stories and people are very romantic YES ☐ NO ☐.

NAME _____ (PLEASE PRINT)

ADDRESS _____

CITY _____ STATE _____ ZIP _____ RS-1

Mail this postage-free card today!

the time her brain was busily composing a note for Hortense, and she needed no distraction, but she couldn't help it. He sat leaning forward on that hard chair, with the sun slanting in on him from the balcony, etching his profile in gold. He took the photographs the old woman passed to him, and perhaps he had seen them all—or something like them—before, but he regarded each one quite seriously, and commented, in Russian or French, making the old lady chuckle with delight until tears ran down her cheeks.

'You are wicked, young man. I should not allow you to talk to me so, but ah! you are doing me good.'

Sacha had heard enough. She slipped away to the bathroom, her plan complete in her mind. She tore the sheet of paper in two—for he was going to search that bathroom, and he would probably find the note—so she would let him. Because when he went to the bathroom, then she would hide the second, duplicate note in the kitchen, in the place that Hortense would definitely find it first thing in the morning—the coffee percolator.

Sacha wrote carefully and clearly. It was difficult not to make the note alarming, but she tried, and was fairly satisfied with the result when at last she slipped the first, 'red herring' letter under a pile of towels in the airing cupboard. She put the second one down her bra and went back into the living room, her pulse beating fast with excitement.

Regretfully at last, Tor looked at his watch, then at Sacha. 'I am afraid we must soon be going,' he said.

Tante Marie's face crumpled like a child's. 'But you must have some wine before you go. I cannot allow you to leave without a drink. Sacha?'

'Yes, of course.'

The ceremony took several minutes. The red wine glowed in the glasses, and they drank it, sweet and delicious, with tiny dry biscuits and petits fours.

'Don't you smoke, young man?' Tante Marie demanded suddenly. Tor lifted a puzzled eyebrow.

'Yes. But I——' he shrugged.

'Then get them out! I would like one with my wine!' She laughed at the expression he could not hide. 'You think I am a bad old woman! Pah! You have seen nothing yet. Tell me—you will come again to see me soon?'

'I would be delighted, *madame*,' he said gravely as he lit the Gauloise for her and looked round for an ashtray.

Sacha jumped up. 'I'll get it, I saw one in the kitchen.' Now was her chance, and she took it. When she returned a moment later the deed was done, and the feeling of relief was so overwhelming that she had to school the expression on her face.

When at last he went to the bathroom, Tante Marie leaned over to grasp Sacha's hand and pull her towards her.

'He is a fine one, that man. You will bring him again? He has made me feel forty years younger!'

Sacha swallowed. She smiled, and it hurt her to tell the lie. 'Of course—I'll try.'

'Don't let him go, eh? There aren't many like him.'

No, there aren't, Sacha agreed silently, and hated herself for what she intended to do. But there was no choice, and Tante Marie would be shocked beyond measure if she knew what her golden boy really was.

At last they left, and were at the bottom, just stepping out into the sunshine, when Tor patted his pocket and said something, very briefly, in Russian. 'Ah, my cigarettes and lighter! I have left them on the table. Wait there. I shall only be a moment.'

Sacha stepped outside and looked up at the flower-strewn balcony. Tante Marie waved. She wouldn't get very far if she made a run for it now, she thought suddenly—and what would the old lady think? 'He has gone back for his cigarettes,' she called.

'Good. They are here—yes.' She had leaned inside the darkened entranceway for a moment, and Sacha breathed slowly. Had he gone back for another look in the bathroom? Could it be possible he hadn't found the first note? She had had to use eyebrow pencil for them, because the other was broken. Perhaps he had assumed she would not bother. Sacha looked up, shading her eyes from the sun as if she would know what he was doing. Tante Marie was talking to him now, and she heard his fainter, deep tones in reply. Then, to her relief, he was there on the balcony, taking the cigarettes and lighter from the old woman, bending over to hold her hand and kiss her cheek. His gesture was sudden and unexpected, and Sacha bit her lip. Oh, why did he have this charm, this ability to do things that could almost bring a lump to her throat? She turned away and watched a red Volkswagen manoeuvre into a space between their motorbike and a Renault. Children's voices carried from a playground nearby, and from the distance came the heavy rumble of traffic, and she looked up again, and he had vanished, and Tante Marie was saying: 'Come again soon.'

Then he was back beside her on the pavement, and she waved, and so did he, and Tante Marie watched them seat themselves on the motorbike. Sacha knew that their visit had made the old woman's day, and she had a faint sick feeling inside her at the thought of the note, and what would happen.

He was silent on the road back to La Valaise. They stopped to buy food, which he loaded into the panniers on the back, and set off again. Sacha held tightly to him when they reached the turn off from the main road, and prepared for a bumpy ride. Suddenly, when they were half way up and could see nothing but the high crumbling walls either side, he stopped. And she knew why—or thought she did, but it wasn't quite the same thing.

'Get off,' he said, and she did so, trying to remember that she was going to have to look very shocked and dismayed in a moment.

'You know why I have stopped?' he demanded.

'Is there something wrong with the engine?' she asked innocently.

'Sometimes my hands itch to spank you. I told you to behave yourself—and what happens?' he brought out her folded note from his pocket, and opened it, reading: 'Hortense. Go to the police and tell them I am held prisoner by three Russians at La Valaise. Do *not* tell Tante Marie. Sacha.' And she had written underneath: 'Urgent—believe me.'

She bit her lip and hung her head. If only she could squeeze a few tears out... She could. And did, and looked up again, her eyes filled with them. 'Oh—oh!' she shook her head from side to side. 'Don't hit me, please,' and she backed slightly and managed a look of utter fear.

He drew in his breath sharply between his teeth, but he didn't seem very angry. 'Don't hit me,' he mimicked her voice and expression with credible accuracy. 'If you act like that I shall be tempted, believe me!'

Sacha waited, and stared at him. He took his lighter from his pocket and flicked it to light a corner of the paper. He held it until she thought it must burn his fingers, then stamped on the black ash.

And then—and then—without a change of expression he took out the second note from his shirt pocket. Now he was watching Sacha's face quite intently, and she didn't need to act this time. She felt the world start to spin round and thought for a moment she was about to faint and put her hand out to the pillion seat to steady herself.

'How——' she could barely speak.

'Do you take me for a complete fool?' He was burning that too, and the last morsel of white paper fluttered to the dry stony ground, and she watched it in fascinated horror, saw the blackened charred edges of it, and wanted to be sick.

'Get on the bike,' he said.

She looked at him desperately. 'No!'

'Get on,' he grated. 'You have tried my patience to its limit. I warn you—you would not like to see me lose my temper.'

'I don't care,' she shook her head. And it was true. She was past caring now; a kind of numbness filled her and she looked around in despair, feeling the horrible sensation of having this go on, for ever, and ever ... and anything was better than that. She began to walk up to the house, because there was nowhere else to go—and how could she run away when he had the motorbike, and could follow her wherever she went? Follow her wherever . . .

She was jerked backwards and pulled round to face him. 'Get on the bike,' he said softly.

Her eyes met his. 'It's a good job Tante Marie can't see you now,' she said. 'She *liked* you. No, I won't get on. I'm walking back to the house.'

For a tense few moments they looked at one another in utter silence. Sacha could meet his eyes now, and she wondered, quite dispassionately, what he would do. For now it was almost as if it were all happening to someone else. She felt remote, almost as if in a dream.

'You know I could make you get on if I wished to.'

'Could you? Why don't you, then?' And she smiled at him, and saw a flicker of something in his eyes that made her heart beat faster.

Then he spoke. 'I admire your courage,' he said quietly. There was no sarcasm in his voice. He was serious.

'I'm not frightened of you,' she answered. And it was true. She had gone past fear to something beyond it, after all that had happened.

'I do not intend that you should be,' and the faintest smile touched his mouth as he said it. 'Go —walk if you wish. I will follow.'

Sacha turned away and began to walk up the steep track. Perspiration ran down her face, and she could feel it on her back and legs, and her skin burned with the force of the sun's rays, and she wanted to be in that quiet kitchen drinking something cool more than anything. She heard the engine start up somewhere behind her, but didn't turn round. So she had won a minor victory—and where had it got her? He was revving up now, as if waiting for her to go farther on before he set off. Sacha walked slowly. Partly because the heat was too intense to do otherwise, partly because she felt sure it would annoy him.

It was tea time, and she was hungry, and wondered what was for the meal. Eggs? And where were the other two? Waiting for her to return so they could run and hide upstairs and play chess?

She wished suddenly that she hadn't been so defiant. If she had got on the bike they would be home now. Home! She smiled bitterly. She had called it that! It would never feel like home again —never, *never* again. Not even when Madame Cassel was safely back, and *they* were gone for ever.

She had to stop because a stone was in her sandal. She bent and slipped it off and shook it, and the pebble rolled out. The motorbike began its ascent, and she had a sudden nightmare feeling that he might run her over. It lasted only a second, but left a fluttery sensation in the centre of her spine, and she quickened her steps instinctively, and half turned round to see where he was. She didn't see the pothole. She had carefully avoided it in the car, because it was quite deep, but she was in it before she had fully turned back and she felt herself going down, saw the ground rushing to meet her, and went sprawling, her bag flying away to land on the grass verge. She was too dazed for a few moments to know exactly what had happened. But distantly, it seemed, an engine cut out, and then she was being lifted to her feet by Tor. She looked down, dismayed at the dusty grey marks all down her dress. It was suddenly all too much to bear. Everything was.

'Oh!' she moaned, and burst into tears. He pulled her to him and put his arms round her, and her face was against his chest, and she felt his heartbeats, slow and strong, and wondered why she should feel so comforted when it was this utterly *despicable* man holding her. The sobs gradually subsided, and he said: 'Have you hurt yourself?' She shook her head, her voice muffled as she answered:

'No—I don't think so. My dress——'

'It will wash,' he answered reassuringly. 'It is only dust, nothing nasty.' He still held her, only now he had his hand in her hair and was stroking the back of her neck and it was most soothing, almost enough to make her feel sleepy . . . and tingly. And she was quite horrified to find she was enjoying it, and didn't *want* to move away, even if she could—but she couldn't anyway because he did have a very firm grip, and that fact eased her conscience. She would definitely examine the reasons for her treachery later, but not there, not just then.

'Now. Is that better?'

'No.'

'Why not?' His voice was near her face, and he spoke softly and kissed her ear when he had said it.

'Because my leg hurts now. And I d-didn't say you could k-kiss me.'

'Ssh, don't start crying again. It was only because you were upset. You always kiss babies better when they fall and hurt themselves, you know,' and he could have been laughing, she wasn't sure, and she suddenly knew it was all part of his act again, and pushed him away with all her strength.

'Why do you do that?' He looked hurt and indignant, and Sacha felt as if she were choking.

'You know why! You men are all the same!' She rubbed her ear and glared at him.

'We are not all the same!' He looked down at her leg, frowned, bent slightly and said: 'Lift your skirt.'

'How dare——' she began, and saw him grin. Quickly he leaned forward and lifted the hem from her knee, just a few inches, but it was enough to make her lash out at him so that he had to dodge back to escape. And he was laughing now.

'*Please* look—there is blood all over your dress— that is all. Truly.'

She looked down then, and saw, dismayed, what he had been trying to do. Her knee was grazed, and a patch of red on the white hem of her dress was evidence of his good intentions.

'Oh!' Then she added: 'You could have *said*!'

He lifted his hands in a gesture of hopelessness. 'I tried. Come, ride the bike sidesaddle—yes? Then we must bandage your poor knee.' He took Sacha's hand and walked across to the motorbike with her, bent and picked up her bag, and then helped her on sideways, nicely.

A minute later they were outside the garage at the back of the house. Sacha walked carefully in, holding the dress away from her knee, although the damage was done.

'Sit in the kitchen. We will attend to your leg first, then you must change.'

She was tired of defiance. It had got her precisely nowhere, and perhaps it would be easier to do as he said. She sat down and waited for him to bring out the box of bandages and ointment from the cupboard.

'I can do it,' she told him as he knelt down.

He looked up, gave her a very level glance but said nothing. He cleaned out all the tiny pieces of grit embedded in the skin with a piece of lint, and she watched him, biting her lip to stop the 'ouches' escaping. Once, when she couldn't help it, she exclaimed, and he looked up and smiled.

'You're enjoying yourself, aren't you?' she accused him. 'I can tell by your face.'

'No. But——' he hesitated, then looked up

99

again. 'You asked for it. You wanted to walk—so——' he shrugged.

'I only looked round because I thought you were going to try and run me over,' she retorted, trying to get back at him. She succeeded only too well. She saw his face change and darken as he looked up at her. He stopped what he was doing.

'Did you think that? Did you really think that?' he asked, and his face was quiet, and it would have been better if he had shouted, for she sensed a smouldering, quick, explosive anger, and regretted her words.

She swallowed hard. 'No,' she answered hesitantly. 'Only for a—a moment. I didn't really. I'm sorry.'

'As you should be.' He was still angry. Really angry, almost white with temper, and she couldn't think why her words should have made him so. The rest of the bandaging was accomplished in a silence which she did not dare to break. Her heart beat faster than usual, and she wondered again at the change in him from what he had been at the old lady's flat.

Immediately he had finished she stood up. 'Thank you. I'll go and change.' He turned away without answering and went to the sink to wash his hands. Sacha hesitated a moment, then went out.

She changed into a cool blue sleeveless top and matching trews, washed the white dress in the bathroom and took it downstairs and outside to hang out. Going inside again she didn't know what to do. Tor was moving about in the kitchen and she didn't want to go there until he had left. But would he? And she was both hungry and thirsty, but her pride wouldn't allow her to go begging to *him*.

The floor was dusty. Odd spent matches and toffee papers littered it. Sacha looked round. She knew where the broom was, and it would be something to do. She went and fetched it out, and the shovel, from the cupboard by the back door, and began to sweep moving the chairs as she went along. She was quite engrossed in her task, and had almost finished when something made her look up to see Tor standing in the kitchen doorway watching her.

'I have made tea,' he said. 'Are you not thirsty?'

'Er—yes, but——'

'Then come and get it.' He turned away without waiting for an answer. Sacha put the broom against the wall, next to the shovel, and followed him out. She sat meekly down at the table, knowing better than to speak, yet scarcely able to bear the oppressive silence that existed. Then, unable to bear it any longer, she burst out: 'I was just sweeping the floor—it looked untidy.'

He lit a cigarette and put the lighter on the table. 'So?'

She looked at him. 'I just thought I'd tell you.'

'And now you have.' He went to the window and

stood with his back to her, beaker of tea in one hand, cigarette in the other. He stood like a soldier, his back very straight, head held high. And Sacha began to realise that she didn't know him, she didn't know this man at all. But then, the thought came, disturbingly, why should she want to?

It grew hotter with the evening, warm and heavy. Sacha had completely lost her appetite, and managed only a piece of bread and some cheese and one or two olives. Tor made no comment as he ate his own larger meal of ham omelette, bread, cheese and wine. She wondered what the other two men were doing. She had heard voices when she was washing her dress before, and it was odd, but it was almost as though there were more than two, but it could have been a radio.

She could see that Tor felt the heat as well. He pulled his shirt loose, and undid the buttons of it as he finished eating. Sacha took his plate and carried it to the sink with her own. There was plenty of hot water in the kettle and she had nothing else to do with her time.

She thought longingly of being able to change into a swimsuit, and the idea brought an unwilling smile to her face. What would *he* say if she did? And oh, for a swim? She had not been in the Mediterranean for a year, but the memories were clear of that smooth greeny-blue water caressing and soft, clear as crystal . . .

'I want to go swimming,' she said suddenly—and surprised herself. She hadn't known she was going to say it until she actually did.

'Ah, you do?' He had his feet up on the table, chair tipped back, and he was trying to blow smoke rings at the light. She looked at him for a moment, wondering how she could ever have thought what a gentleman he was at Tante Marie's. Loathing filled her. And to think she had actually *enjoyed* being in his arms after she had fallen! She went hot and cold at the thought, and the skin on the back of her neck crawled at the memory of his caressing touch.

'Yes, I do.' Her voice was firmer. 'It's too hot to do anything else. And I don't suppose I'd be allowed to wander off to Cannes to enjoy the night life, would I?'

'How very clever of you.' He examined his left thumbnail carefully, and Sacha, by a great effort of will, prevented herself from kicking the legs of his chair from under him. For some reason he was still smouldering, but whether it was because of her remark about him running her over, or for some other reason, she could not be sure—and the last thing she would dare do would be to ask.

'Do you think you deserve to go?' he said suddenly.

'No.' Sacha's eyes sparkled defiance. 'But I do know that if you hadn't been here and ruined my holiday, I would have been able to go swimming just when I wanted—without having to ask.'

The muscles tightened in his jaw, and she wondered why he was still angry.

'Very well.' He looked at his watch. 'We shall go.'

She didn't believe him. She made no move, just looked at him in silence, and he uncurled himself slowly from his reclining position, and stood up, towering over her, making the room seem smaller by comparison.

'I will get the motorbike—or do you prefer to walk?'

It was a mile down to the main road, another five minutes to the beach—and which was preferable, walking with him in stony silence, or having to hold him tight?

'Let's walk.' She remembered her manners. 'Please.'

'As you wish.' He inclined his head slightly. And when she still made no move, in case she had imagined it all, he added softly: 'Do you swim with no clothes on?'

The question was so surprising that she felt herself go pink. 'No!'

'Then why do you not go and get your costume?'

'Oh—yes.' She went quickly out, feeling foolish and annoyed. He followed her a moment later and she heard him go into the other room and say something to the two men. She heard their answering voices, quieter, more distant, then he was shutting the door and walking along the landing. Sacha hurriedly turned and bent to her case—still un-

104

packed—and felt for her white swimsuit and towel. Shutting the door and bolting it, she undressed and put the suit on, slipped trousers and top over it and ran down again.

He was at the door waiting, a denim jacket over his arm, a look of cool disinterest on his face. And Sacha suddenly felt miserable. In spite of everything, he could be good company—had been only hours before on the visit to Tante Marie. It could almost be enjoyable now—almost—if only he would drop that stony cold *remoteness*.

As they set out, she asked him: 'Aren't you going to swim?'

'No.' The answer, monosyllabic, was discouraging, but she persisted.

'Why not?'

'I do not choose to.'

'And—and are you also going to keep silent all the way there and back?' she asked, made reckless by the warmth, and the night, and a thousand other things that she didn't understand.

'I think it better. Every time we speak—we fight. So——' he shrugged, striding out down the track so that she had to hurry to keep pace with him, '—if I keep quiet, no fights. Then *you* are happy.'

She couldn't tell him just how unhappy she was. 'All right,' she answered. '*Thanks* so much for telling me.' The icy sarcasm was probably lost on him, for he showed not a flicker of reaction.

After that they didn't speak at all. It was strange,

she thought, most odd to be walking down through France's most stunningly beautiful countryside to a secluded beach for a swim. With the right man it could be too romantic for words. The right man. Who was he? Not Nigel—Nigel, the man she had come here to forget. Well, that had worked anyway. Yes, she thought, I can certainly recommend being held prisoner by three mad Russians as a cure for a broken heart. Her natural exuberance was reasserting itself. So he wouldn't speak. Fine. She would think instead. She tried to think of Nigel. What was he doing now? He knew where she was, and probably imagined her to be having a gay whirl of a time, meeting people, going to parties. It would be almost funny if it wasn't so horribly untrue. Nothing could be further from that than what was happening now; being guarded virtually day and night by this Russian *bear*. This fiery, unpredictable, charming, steel-*hard* man.

Sacha risked a sideways glance at him. She had never met a man so tough-looking, so uncompromisingly strong. And then she wondered—perhaps he couldn't *swim*. She bit her lip to stop a laugh escaping. That would be funny indeed, if this karate expert couldn't do anything more than paddle in the shallows. Why else would he refuse the chance for a swim on a hot sticky night with the moon a huge silver orb low in the sky to light the way, and the sea a soft warm bed to lie in? She wouldn't ask—she would not dare—but she was to find out the answer, although then, walking down that stony track, she couldn't have guessed just how.

The beach was only tiny, surrounded by rocks so that if you didn't know about it, you wouldn't find it.

They scrambled down the last few yards of rocky incline and Tor looked round, but said nothing. The worst part of their journey had been crossing the busy main road, always worse at night because of the speed at which the cars travelled. He had taken her arm briefly as they ran across, but moved his hand the moment they reached the other side.

Now, on the beach, he spoke. 'I will sit here,' he pointed to a flat rock that sloped gently upwards at such an angle as to provide a good back rest. 'You will go and swim, and you will stay where I can see you. You understand?'

'Only too well,' she answered. 'You have a way of making yourself perfectly clear even if you are speaking a different language from your own.' But if she had hoped to provoke him—and she wasn't sure about it—he showed no sign, merely sat down and leaned against the rock and began feeling for his cigarettes.

Sacha slipped off the top and trousers and ran down to the waiting sea without a backward glance. Slender, beautiful and long-legged in the white swim-suit that almost shimmered in the moonlight, she was quite unaware of the stunningly attractive picture she made—nor that the man called Tor watched her because he found it too difficult to tear his eyes from her.

The water lapped softly round her feet—legs—waist, and she shivered, but it was from pleasure, not cold, for it was as marvellous and tingling as ever. With a little sigh she fell forward and then turned on her back to float and look up at the sky, dark and thickly diamond-studded. Her hair spread out like a fan, and she winced for her so recent set —but what did it matter now?

She turned and did a lazy crawl out to sea, and a piece of seaweed floated past and touched her arm in a wet caress, and she jumped.

Then she saw the yacht, and stopped swimming to tread water while she looked hungrily at it. It was moored out to sea, a good half mile out, but it was ablaze with light from every possible space, and the music that had been too faint was now clear. She even recognised the tune, an old Beatles number, 'Yesterday'—slightly sad. There were people on board, perhaps dozens of them, enjoying themselves, drinking, dancing, talking—laughing.

Sacha looked back, wondering if *he* had seen. But the angle of the rocks hid him. And it was at that moment that the idea began to form in Sacha's mind. Could she do it? Could she *swim* to it? Could she? She was very still in the water all of a sudden, treading slowly and lazily to conserve all her energy. For it needed thought. Distance was deceptive at sea, especially in moonlight, and that half mile might be more, and she had only swum half a mile at her best. And she thought, and watched the lights and their reflections in the still dark waters as the boat bobbed very gently, and the music changed and was now 'Bridge over Troubled Water,' and that was all she needed to decide her. All she needed. Taking a deep breath, Sacha struck out towards that white yacht, her port in the storm she was in.

She heard a faint voice calling from the beach, Tor, and looked back.

'Come in!' he shouted, and she waved as if that was what she intended to do, then dived under-water to swim until her lungs were bursting. And she was that much further away from him now, and it didn't matter, because he *couldn't swim*.

The music was so much louder, floating clearly over the water, carrying in the still warm air, and it was beautiful and soothing to listen to because her arms were getting tired and the song was keeping her going, and she wondered what Tor was doing *now* and paused to look back. But he wasn't there. Something prickled at the back of Sacha's neck, a presentiment of danger, and she trod water to rest her arms for a moment. Then she saw the move-ment in the sea between her and the beach, saw the dark shiny head, the faint white foam—and she knew where he was.

CHAPTER FIVE

PANICKING, Sacha turned and struck out towards those welcoming lights and sounds, and her heart was nearly bursting with the supreme effort. But she was nearer now. Near enough to see a couple standing on deck kissing each other, two tiny figures lost in a world of their own, and she put her head down, breathe in—out—in—keep going, *keep going*—don't stop . . .

Something grabbed her arm, and it wasn't seaweed, but she was too exhausted to shout, then Tor's voice came in her ear and she felt his body beside her in the water, and heard him say:

'If you make a sound I will knock you unconscious. You hear me?' His hand was on her neck, and she knew about pressure points, knew he could do it if he wanted to—and that he would if he had to.

Her tired lungs grabbed air as she felt herself going down and was pulled sharply up. 'Lie on your back.'

'No,' she whispered. 'I only wanted to get there.' She reached out her arm to push him away, but it was like pushing at a shiny hard wall.

'Stop struggling—lie flat, I am going to take you to shore. Float on your back.'

She knew it was no use fighting, had known all along, but something had made her keep on trying. But now was too much. She had tried and failed again, and this time she had no strength left to argue. She turned over on her back, felt his body beneath her, his hands under her arms, and she lay passively as he kicked out with his feet. Gradually strength returned and she tried to shift his grip and swim on her own. They were further away from the yacht, the music was faint and somehow sad, and she pushed his hands away. 'Let me swim on my own. *Leave* me.'

He struck out beside her and paced her, and they neared the shore. It was all she could do to swim at all now. Each leg movement was such an effort that it hurt, and her arms were on fire, every fibre of muscle protesting. But she would not, she would *not* let him see. In, out, breathe in, breathe out, it was almost a chant as they neared shore—and then she felt solid sand beneath her legs and fell the last few feet, stumbled, crawled and finally dragged herself on to the thick white crunchy sand and rolled over on her back.

The next moment Tor flung himself on her. She felt his hard body on top of her, winding her, the weight of him knocking nearly all the breath out of her exhausted body.

'Let——' that was all she was allowed to say before his lips came down on hers in a brutally savage hungry kiss that took the last vestiges of her breath away. She was utterly stunned, completely helpless, lying there beneath him—and it was like the other time in the bedroom, and she stirred then at the memory and tried to push him away.

'No—Tor—stop——' His answer was to take her hair in his free hand so that her head stayed still, and kiss her again violently.

Excitement stirred inside her. In spite of everything, she felt a treacherous warmth fill her body as his touch burned her like fire, and they were locked together in an embrace that went on and on until he had to stop for breath—and a vestige of sanity returned to Sacha and she opened her eyes and drew a long shuddering breath.

She was weak, but she had enough strength to lift her hand to her face and cover her mouth. As he tried to take it away she breathed: 'Tor—you're hurting me—please——'

He rolled off and came to his feet, yanking her to hers with one swift movement. His chest heaved and his voice was harsh, his accent stronger than ever as he ground out: 'I would like to *beat* you!'

Sacha jerked her hand free and rubbed her wrist. '*That* wasn't what you were trying to do just then.' Her voice trembled and shook.

'No——' he ran his fingers through his soaking hair. 'Go and get dressed—now.'

'But I'm not dry——' she began. He pulled her savagely along to the place where she had left her clothes. His shirt and sandals were lying on the sand beside them. He picked up her towel and flung it at her.

'Do not speak to me—do not answer me back—just dry yourself,' he ordered. 'You have done enough tonight. Believe me, you will regret it if you try and fight me now.' He was a lithe bronzed giant, in a towering rage, and capable of she knew not what, and a ripple of fear ran through Sacha. All the veneer of civilisation was stripped off; underneath was the primitive man who had so brutally attacked her. Her mouth, her whole body, still ached from the embrace—and she knew suddenly that it had affected him too, for he would not be still, but moved restlessly, vibrant, poised ready for action, a coiled spring of high tension.

Her heartbeats were coming back to normal now. She towelled herself, glad of the action to stop her thinking, rubbing her hair, flinging it back, bending to dry her legs and feet, nearly overbalancing as she did so. Then she put the towel down and picked up her trousers and slid them over the damp suit. She sneezed and began to shiver, for the air felt cooler, and he saw her and said:

'Take off your swim costume. We have a long walk.'

'Not with *you* here.'

'I will turn round. Do as I say.'

She swallowed hard and walked behind the jutting out rocks and quickly slipped off her soaking, clinging suit. He stood with his back to her, looking out to sea restlessly, and she put on her top and trews and stepped out into the open.

'I'm ready.' He turned slowly round.

'Then we will go.'

'Don't you want to get dry?' Not that she really cared. All she could feel now was a sick disappointment at her failure to reach the yacht. That, and a kind of growing dismay at what had happened on the beach, at the edge of the water. For something could no longer be denied. He had done it to punnish her, she knew—the kisses had, in a strange way been for him the only alternative to physical violence. But for her they had triggered off something she had thought dead after she had finished with Nigel—an awareness of herself as a woman, and of her feelings.

'No, I will dry myself as we go along. Come.' He picked up his shirt and jacket—slid his knife, keys and wallet into his back pocket and put his watch on. Sacha looked at him. In between deciding to go after her and actually doing so, he had carefully taken off the things that would get damaged or lost. And she had decided he couldn't even swim!

She threw the towel at him and began scrambling up the rocky face to the top, leaving him to follow. She carried her well wrung out suit over one arm, and made it to the top fairly easily, although now she was regretting that they had not brought the motorbike.

She was warmer again with the wet suit off, and

if only her legs felt a bit stronger the walk back wouldn't be too bad. They neared the road, and she had to stop. Cars whizzed past in both directions, lights brilliant searchlights stabbing the black road ahead, sweeping past at anything up to a hundred miles an hour, sports cars, sleek Rolls-Royces, the occasional caravan behind family saloons, all with a destination—somewhere to go. She stood quite still, aware of the man beside her, not looking at him, though. She felt very tired, almost ill, and was suddenly frightened that she wouldn't be able to cross the road.

'Now—quickly.' He pulled her half way across, and they waited in that perilously narrow centre strip to allow a Peugeot to speed past. Then safely at the other side he took his hand away. He had been angry before they had even left the house. So what was he like now? Far worse, undoubtedly, and Sacha began to get the nightmare feeling all over again. Would it ever end?

It always seemed, with each hour that passed, as if freedom became even more remote than before.

All her spirit was gone. The swim to the yacht had been her last attempt at escape, although he wouldn't know that. She couldn't walk fast, and she knew by the way he kept looking back and waiting that he thought she was doing it deliberately. Her legs felt very heavy after the salty buoyancy of the water, and it was all she could do to keep one leg following the other steadily upwards, up to the house which had changed beyond all measure in just two days, and would never be the same again.

A rabbit scuttered across the path ahead of them and vanished into the undergrowth at the side of the path. Faintly behind them from the road a horn blared, long and impatient. And that was all. The rest of the journey took place in silence.

When they got into the house a strange thing happened. As Tor bolted the door after them, one of the men called from upstairs to him. He looked at Sacha, handed her the towel and said: 'Wait here,' and ran upstairs, taking them two at a time. She stood quite still, listening, heard voices, then the door closed upstairs and they were cut off. It was unbelievable, but it had seemed as if he was speaking *English*. Yet neither of the men spoke it.

She went quickly into the kitchen, warmed some milk, beat a raw egg, and poured the warm milk on. The pain inside her was partly caused by hunger, and yet she didn't want solid food.

After putting the towel and swimsuit to soak she sat at the table and drank the egg in milk. Then she waited for Tor to come down. When several minutes had gone by with no sign of him, she crept upstairs and into bed, and she was too tired to care that she had disobeyed him, too tired to care if she made him angry again. He could hardly be worse than he had already been.

When she woke up she didn't know where she was.

She was still sobbing from an awful dream of being completely lost in a strange land, peopled by weird gnomelike creatures who vanished if you looked at them. The dream was so real and vivid that she sat up, putting her hand to her burning forehead, wondering if she had gone mad. Her breath came quickly and shakily as she fought to get back to normal.

Then she remembered. And the reality was even worse than the dream. She looked across at the other bed in the room—and Tor was lying there watching her. Sacha covered her mouth to stop the gasp of dismay escaping. She saw him move, then: 'What is the matter?' he said.

'N-nothing.' Then, as he made as if to sit up: 'No—please—no, leave me.'

He was abruptly still. 'I was not going to touch you. I was going down to get you a drink. You need one. You have been calling out for a few minutes.'

'I'll go down. I'd rather. Please let me.'

'Very well. There is brandy in the cupboard. It will settle your nerves.'

She padded barefoot downstairs, switching on the light as she went. The clock said four, and it was still dark. As she crossed the living room to the kitchen, she heard a noise outside, and froze. Then she looked at the front door—and it was unbolted. And it was being *opened*—very slowly.

She screamed for Tor—she remembered doing that afterwards—and began to run to the stairs.

Half way up, and Tor was coming down two at a time, and then was holding her, pushing her behind him so that his way was clear to—and a tall young man walked in and said in an American drawl:

'Hi! Why all the lights? You miss me or somethin'?'

She heard Tor swear in Russian. She didn't know Russian—but she knew swearing when she heard it, and the young American looked at her, raised his eyebrows and said: 'Did I do something wrong? I only went out to check up.'

'You just nearly made Sacha die of fright,' Tor said. '*That* is all.'

Sacha sat on the stairs. Her legs would not have carried her either up or down and it seemed the best place to be. At least the mystery of the voices was solved, but it left other much more urgent questions unanswered.

'I'm sorry, honey. Really. You going to introduce us, Tor?'

Tor turned round, looked at her. 'Sacha, this is Wayne O'Malley. He is from America. Wayne, Miss Sacha Donnelly.'

The American came forward and stuck out his hand. He was in his late twenties, quite as tall as Tor, in a lean, clean-cut Yankee way, and pleasantly good-looking with light brown curly hair and laughing eyes.

'I'm sure sorry we met like this, honey. I've gotten a lot of explaining to do—but I didn't know I'd be doing it at four in the morning——'

Tor interrupted. 'I do not think that now is the time either, eh, Wayne? She is tired. We are all tired, yes?'

'Wait a minute,' said Sacha. It was the first time she had spoken since she had screamed Tor's name in her fear, and both men stopped talking to look at her. 'I think that now is the time—yes,' she said. 'If you think I'm just going b-back to bed——' She stopped.

Tor looked at her and frowned. He had changed into his shorts, and over them wore a white tee-shirt that made him look more broad-shouldered than ever. His feet were bare—but then, she thought, he'd hardly had time to put anything on them, the way she had screamed.

'You need brandy. Come—sit in this chair. Not on the cold stairs. You will take cold.' She pulled away as he would have taken her arm, and came slowly down the stairs, little realising the picture she made. Her hair tousled after the swim, her face pale with fatigue and shock, eyes wide and frightened, she was a fragile, delicately appealing figure, walking with dignity to the easy chair, her feet bare, her trouser suit rumpled with sleep, and yet there was an unmistakable quiet femininity about her that kept both men's eyes riveted to her. When she sat, Tor went out to the kitchen and returned with three glasses and a bottle which he set down

119

on the table. Wordlessly, he poured the amber liquid.

While he was doing this, Sacha sat quietly, her hands on her knee, wondering just how much more she was expected to take—and whether she could. Tor handed her a glass half full of brandy.

'I don't want that much,' she said quietly.

'Yes. It will not hurt you.' Then, when she looked up, he added: 'Please, Sacha.' He wasn't angry any more. There was nothing of the previous fury in his eyes now. He looked almost gentle, and his hair was spiky because of the way it had dried after his swim, and his face was dark with stubble because he had a heavy beard, and Sacha's heart lurched slightly . . .

'Cheers, Sacha.' Wayne raised his glass. 'May I call you that? I feel as if I know you—I've got something to tell you. I'll make it snappy because it's the middle of the night, and explanations can wait till morning. I had your passport, and I've brought it back. I'm sorry we had to pinch it, but we wanted to check out that you were who you said you were.'

She looked up at him, but said nothing. It wasn't making sense—yet. The reason was because of the old man staying here. What did you call him?' he looked at Tor. 'Serge?' Tor nodded.

'Well, his name's not Serge. It's Igor Maievsky—Professor Maievsky—he defected ten days ago—' but Sacha stopped listening. She knew now where she had seen that face. It had been in the newspapers just over a week ago when a top Russian scientist had vanished during a conference in East Berlin. Disappeared into thin air, and nobody knew where—but now she did.

'And Tor and Janos have been guarding him here—only Janos slipped up one day. Went for a shower and the old man remembered he wanted cigars and ran to catch up with Tor because he heard his bike stop. And he saw you—and you saw him.'

Sacha had just had a swallow of the cognac. The room started to swim round and she put the glass down quickly on the table. She heard Wayne's voice, but it was far away, and the rushing sound in her ears was louder and louder, and she heard only —'she's fainted', before she did. She didn't know which of them said it, and she didn't care.

She lay in bed feeling the cold soft cloth wiping her face until she pushed it away. It was Tor sitting on the bed leaning over her, Tor holding the damp flannel. She turned her head away from him and prayed for him to go and leave her alone. Tears filled her eyes.

'Sacha?' he spoke softly. 'Are you awake?' When she didn't answer he touched her face gently and turned it to him. 'You fainted and now you are in bed. Do you want anything?'

She shook her head. He stood up. 'I will go now. Sleep well,' and he went out. She lay there quite still and quiet. She was so very tired, completely exhausted, that she could hardly think. But one thing stood out clear and strong. Tor was no criminal. Neither were the others. Everything fell into place with a startling suddenness. Then she remembered the touch of Tor's lips on hers and that lovely warm glow filled her again. And it was with that memory that she fell asleep.

They were eating breakfast—all five of them, together—and Janos really wasn't as bad as she had first feared. Tor and Wayne were cooking ham and eggs and fresh-picked mushrooms. They would not allow her to do a thing, and she sat at the table like a queen, with the gentle professor at one side of her, Tor translating anything he said, and the atmosphere was different. Before there had been tension everywhere. Now it had gone, and in its place had come calm, and some laughter.

Tor was an expert chef. That had been obvious to Sacha when she first came, and he had that air of enjoying it too. She ate well, really hungry now after all that had happened.

She had brushed her hair back so that it hung straight and shiny down her back, and she wore brief white shorts and a deep blue sleeveless cotton blouse that she knew brought out the colour of her eyes. If by chance her glance met Tor's there was something in his eyes that brought warmth to her face. Gone the terrible anger, now he too was relaxed, and Sacha saw he was a different man again.

When breakfast was finished, Wayne said: 'Can we go for a little walk later, Sacha? There's a lot of explaining to do, I guess, and Tor thinks you won't believe him.' He looked up and winked at Tor, who turned from the stove as if about to say something, then thinking better of it, gave a crooked smile.

'Yes, of course,' agreed Sacha. 'I must go up first to make my bed. I won't be long.'

She was standing by her bed, thinking about everything, just about to smooth the covers over when there was a knock at the door and Tor's voice came: 'May I come in, Sacha?'

'Yes.' She turned to face him, and he shut the door behind him.

'I have come to say that I am sorry for what I did—on the beach—last night.'

'Oh,' she looked away quickly, confused, remembering. 'It—it doesn't matter.'

'Yes, it does.' He came forward and touched her arm very gently. 'I behaved very badly. I was very angry, but that is no excuse, I know.'

'I understand now why it was so essential that I didn't tell anyone,' she said slowly. 'If only you had told *me* in the beginning!'

'Yes, but we could not. You see, I did not *know* who you were—even though you told me. We had to be sure. And until we were I had to watch you. That is why'—he nodded towards his own bed—'I had to stay. That was not nice for you either, I know, but it is over now. You will be able to sleep in peace tonight.'

Her breathing was very shallow as she asked the next, inevitable question. 'When will you be leaving, Tor?'

He shrugged. 'As soon as ever possible. Then you can have your holiday, doing what *you* wish to do.'

'I see.' How could she tell him what was in her heart—that a holiday now, alone, would be a mere shadow of what it could have been? There was an ache inside her, almost a pain, but she could say nothing. 'Well,' she spoke lightly, 'I'd better get on, hadn't I? I'll make your bed as well, after all, you did a lovely breakfast—it's the least I can do.'

'Thank you, Sacha. By the way, I hung out your swimming suit and towel last night. You had left them in the bowl.'

'I forgot them. Thanks.' There was a throbbing tension filling the room quite suddenly, and she could not stand it. She looked at him, and he was aware of it too; it showed in his eyes, on his face—a tingling awareness that reached out and touched them both.

She closed her eyes, and lifted one hand to touch her forehead.

'You are tired?'

'A little,' she admitted. 'I'll be better after a good night's sleep.'

'Yes. So too will I. Well,' he gave her a slight

smile, 'better I go now, I think. I am going to a shop in the village. Is there anything you need?'

She thought—and remembered. 'I never let my father know I had arrived. Could you—would you send a telegram for me?'

'Of course.' He inclined his head. 'Write it out and I will take it for you. There is no hurry, I must feed the hens first.' He turned and went out.

Wayne and Sacha walked as far as Madame Cassel's house and stopped to watch the hens pecking at the feed scattered by Tor for them.

Wayne had been explaining the situation, and she had been listening carefully, knowing, even as she did, that it was too fantastic for words.

'You see, Sacha,' he explained, as they leaned against the rough stone wall of Madame Cassel's little house, 'it was a very tight operation all round. We'd had whispers that Maievsky was intending to defect when he went to East Berlin for this conference. We had to swing into action right away this end—in case he made it—and *how* he made it from East Berlin I'm not allowed to tell you, because the way could possibly be used again. I can tell you this. He arrived in Marseilles a week ago, and was brought straight here.' He paused to offer Sacha a cigarette before lighting one for himself. 'Both Tor and Janos are top bodyguards—but Tor was here mainly because he's trilingual—he's half French, you know, of course.' Sacha didn't know, but she wouldn't have interrupted him for the world. 'I'm here because I'm dealing with the next stage, getting him to America. Tor's work is finished here then—Janos will go with us.'

And she had to ask him then. 'And Tor, what will he do?'

Wayne grinned. 'Go back to his restaurant. He's got one of those places that gets rosettes in all the good food guides—somewhere in the Loire valley, I believe. I've heard the cooking is out of this world. He came over here five years ago, so I guess he's more French than Russian by now.' He paused to flick ash to the ground and tread on it before continuing: 'His wife will be looking after the place while he's away—it's one of those places where you have to book your meal days ahead——' his words were being said, and she heard them, but she wasn't listening. Tor was married. And why not? He was at least thirty. There was nothing unusual about that. But her throat and mouth had gone dry, and there was a stone where her heart should have been, which was strange because it continued beating.

'I didn't know he was married,' she said, very casually.

'Sure. Got a couple of kids too. I've never met them, but word gets around.' So he was a father too. At least Nigel hadn't any children, but it was all the same. They were both the same.

And wasn't it a good job she had found out now,

before she made a complete fool of herself? Sacha gave a small tight smile, desperate to appear normal, and asked: 'Tell me, was anyone watching the house at night? Only we went a walk early one morning—and I had this feeling——'

'We had a couple of men camped out near the farm. They had binoculars—and Tor was in radio contact, of course, most of the time——'

She nodded and smiled in the right places, and listened, but the pain was hard to bear. She had come away to forget Nigel—and very successfully she had done it. The only trouble was she would be going home with another, different ache. How ironic!

'So if I hadn't come at that moment—if I hadn't *seen* Serge—I mean the professor—none of this would have happened?'

'Nope. Oh, we'd probably have tailed you as a precaution, but it wouldn't have been so important. You were just unlucky. I get the—uh—impression from Tor that you—uh—tried to get away a few times.'

She had to smile at his diffident manner. 'What exactly *did* he say?'

Wayne grinned. 'Nope. I'm not going to stir it up for anyone—'specially me! I don't tangle with people like Tor—I prefer them on my side—which is more or less what he said about you.'

'Tell me. I won't say anything,' she breathed.

He shrugged and grinned at her. 'He told me,

amongst other things, that you packed quite a punch for such a dainty-looking creature!'

'Oh,' she wasn't sure why she had wanted to know, after all. What possible interest was it to her now what Tor said or did? 'I suppose,' she said casually, 'he meant the time I tried to knock him out with a wooden pole. Only I missed,' she added.

He looked at her with open admiration. 'Holy cow! You didn't!' He gave a low whistle. 'Boy, I'll bet he was good and mad. Rather you than me, honey.'

'He said—if I'd been a man he might have killed me.'

'And he probably meant it too. I've seen him break a plank of wood in two with the side of his hand.' Then he added: 'Weren't you even *frightened*?'

'Yes,' she admitted. 'At first. But I had to try and get away—don't you see?'

'Sure do, honey. Say, you know, Sacha, you're quite a girl!' he took her arm casually. 'Let's go back. I don't want Tor getting jealous!'

'That's hardly likely,' she answered lightly. 'We don't particularly like one another—and, after all, he is married.'

'Yeah, so he is. But—come on, honey.'

Tor had gone to the village when they returned to the house, and Sacha was glad. It gave her more time to prepare herself. For she was going to be casual, and friendly, and she wasn't going to let anything show, and then he would never guess her feelings, and perhaps after he'd gone, in a day or so, she would be able to forget him. But she knew deep inside her that she wouldn't.

When he did return, loaded up with food, he caught her alone in the kitchen and handed her a small parcel. 'This is for you Sacha,' he said, and bowed—and it was the most natural thing in the world for him to do.

'Thank you.' She took it carefully, hiding her surprise. It was quite heavy. 'Can I open it now?'

'Of course,' he grinned, and her heart gave a funny lurch. Did he do it deliberately? Didn't he *know* what effect it had on her?

She sat down and began to open the well wrapped package to reveal at last, in a small box, an exquisite glass paperweight of the kind known as *mille fiore*—only there was only one flower inside, an exquisite rose with one leaf, caught in the centre of the glass, imprisoned for ever—and beautiful too, for ever.

'It's lovely, thank you, Tor,' she breathed. She mustn't cry. She mustn't. She smiled at him, and the look in his eyes sent the blood rushing to her face, so that she had to look quickly down at the paperweight. She stroked its cool smoothness gently.

'I'll go and pack it away somewhere safe—I don't want it to get broken,' she said, and put it in the box. 'Excuse me.' She had to pass him, and he didn't move aside as he would have done normally, so that their bodies touched, and the contact sent an exquisite pain through her. As she went into her bedroom and closed the door, Sacha made her decision. She was going to avoid being alone with Tor as much as possible in the time remaining, and if he didn't understand why, it was just too bad. She wasn't even going to think about how he, a married man, could enjoy making advances to her as he had. Did he never have twinges of guilt? she wondered. Perhaps it didn't matter. The Frenchman made a notoriously fickle husband, and perhaps, having lived there for several years, and being half French, he qualified as one.

Sacha went to her car and brought out her paints and canvases. She had rigged up an easel before with the aid of a kitchen chair and a tray, and as she went into the living room from the kitchen, carrying them, she saw Wayne coming down the stairs.

'Hi!' he greeted her. 'Hey, let me help,' he grinned at her, and took the chair and tray from her. 'Where to?'

'The garden at the front, please. Where is everyone?'

'Upstairs, going over the final plans. It's tonight or early tomorrow morning.'

'Oh, I see.' And then she wouldn't see Tor again. And the thought was awful, but she was going to bear it, because there was no choice.

He set the things down near her paints. 'Uh-huh.

Want me to fix your easel up?'

She smiled at him. 'How did you guess?'

'They don't call me Brains O'Malley for nothing, hon. What are you going to sit on?'

'Oh, a smaller chair from the living room. I'll go and get it.'

Tor was coming down the stairs. She looked up.

'May I borrow your car in the morning, Sacha? I will bring Madame Cassel back home in it if I can.'

'Yes, of course. But what will you tell her? I thought you'd rented this place for another week or two.'

'Yes, but I did explain to her that we might have to leave before, and that I would let her know—because of the hens. Do not worry, I will explain the mix-up of the missing letter, and that you came, and all is well.'

He thinks of everything, thought Sacha bitterly. Everything except how to stop a stupid English girl from falling in love with him. I wish I still hated him, like I did at the beginning. It would make everything so much easier. But she didn't, she knew that now—if indeed she ever had. She would remember the impact that that first sight of him had been. She would never forget that lithe smiling giant striding towards the car from his machine, for he had looked stunningly attractive. Then and now. She watched him as he turned to go into the kitchen, then stopped and said to her: 'I will make coffee for us all, I think. You would like one, Sacha?'

'Please.' Oh yes, he was stunning all right. No wonder Tante Marie had fallen too! He could charm the birds off the trees if he felt so inclined. And she remembered her resolution, and picked up the chair, and carried it outside, and if she was having to blink, it was only, she told herself, because the sun stung her eyes.

Sacha spent the rest of the day in the garden, at first in the sun, sketching the house, then later, as it grew too warm, in the shade of the pines. It was better this way. Safer too. She didn't even go in for lunch, but ate sandwiches outside on the grass. Let the men talk among themselves, and make their plans. She had no part in those, no part at all.

When it grew night she went into the house, reluctantly, because she could hardly sit out there painting in the dark.

The men were in the living room playing poker, and she suddenly had the awful feeling of being completely excluded from the little party, an oddly disturbing sensation.

'Please don't get up,' she breathed, as she saw Tor and Wayne about to rise to their feet. 'I'll just sit and watch for a while.'

'You wish to play?' Tor asked her. She shook her head.

'I always lose at cards. I'd rather watch, really.' She could smell something cooking in the kitchen.

Carefully she put the damp canvas down on the table in the corner of the room, then her paints, so that they would be out of the way.

She wondered when the men would leave—and how—and then she realised that Tor would not be going with them. She sat very still on her chair at the edge of the table, between Wayne and Janos, and she thought about that. Tor was staying here— and there would then be just the two of them, alone, in the house.

'—fto xxq qirb teuj I bxxa borii yxxv xxxxd xwnd
xur to txxxxq x oi tuxxxoxxi 1I .bxxxxho xi .xoxxx P

CHAPTER SIX

WAYNE vanished upstairs after dinner, and when
he came down he was carrying what looked like a
large modern transistor radio—with too many dials
to be quite ordinary.

'That's it,' he announced. 'Be ready at midnight.
Tor, will you tell them?'

There followed a brief conversation in Russian,
after which Tor brought out glasses and cognac,
and they all had a drink. The room gradually filled
with smoke from the professor's cigars and the
others' cigarettes, and she felt very sleepy. She was
determined to stay awake to say goodbye to the
three men, however, and curled up in the arm-
chair, leaving them to talk among themselves. She
yawned once or twice, and settled herself more
comfortably, and the voices droned and faded, and
blue smoke swirled lazily round in the air . . . It's
like a scene from a film, she thought—and I'm part
of it . . . And then she fell asleep.

Wayne was shaking her arm, and she opened her
eyes in alarm.

'What is it?'

'We're going, honey. Any minute now. It's
nearly twelve.'

Hurriedly she sat up, blinking. 'I'm sorry, I must

have been very tired and I just dropped off—'

'I know,' he grinned, 'it happens to the best of us at times. You looked so peaceful there, snoring your pretty head off—'

'I wasn't, was I?' she exclaimed in horror, and he laughed.

'I'm kidding, Sacha. There wasn't a peep out of you.'

There were only the two of them in the room, and she looked round.

'They're getting their things together. Me, I travel light. Just have what I stand up in to worry about.' And then they heard the noise, and a prickle of excitement teased Sacha's spine. Wayne stood up.

'That's it, I reckon. Come and look.'

She had never seen a helicopter close up. She wished suddenly that she had a camera to snap it, because her father would never have believed it . . . A helicopter in the front garden at La Valaise!

The men ran down the stairs as the clicking rotor blades slowed and stopped, and everything was still. Tor opened the door and waved, and turned to Janos and the professor, saying something in Russian.

Professor Maievsky turned to Sacha and held out his hand.

'Goodbye,' she said softly, 'have a safe journey,' and perhaps he understood, for his smile spoke for him. Janos shook her hand and bowed, Wayne came over and hugged her lightly. 'See you again, Sacha—say, you get your passport back?'

Tor answered for her. 'It is upstairs. I will give it to her later.'

She waited in the doorway and saw the dark figures go outside, the faint light from the cabin of the helicopter showing the shadowy outline of the pilot. Tor reached up to help the men in, final handshakes were exchanged, and then he was ducking back, standing clear as the mighty rotor blades roared into action and lifted the machine, like a giant mosquito, off the ground and into the sky.

It was over. They had gone. And Sacha felt unaccountably sad. She saw Tor give a last wave, the helicopter dipped, then soared off effortlessly, and then he ran back towards the house, and she turned away. She had decided not to be alone with him. But that would be rather difficult now.

It was past twelve, so it was Sunday now. Her first Sunday of the holiday. And she could never have dreamed it would be like this.

Tor came in and bolted the door, then he said: 'Do you want a drink?'

'No, thanks, I'm too tired. I'll go up to bed now.'

'Very well. Goodnight, Sacha.'

'Goodnight, Tor.' He had sobered with their going. He looked tired, as if he too needed sleep. There were faint shadows beneath his eyes, and lines of strain from nose to mouth.

Sacha turned and went slowly up the stairs. After

she had washed she went into her bedroom and, very carefully and quietly, bolted the door.

It was very late when she woke. She knew it first of all by the position of the sun through the window and then by looking at her watch. It was past ten.

The house was silent when she went to the bathroom, and she wondered if he too was still asleep. She hoped he was. She showered and dressed in the plain white shift she had worn for her visit to Tante Marie, and realisation came as she put it on. She was free! Free to go where she pleased—to visit the old lady if she wanted, go for a swim, or walk, or drive into Cannes—or anywhere else for that matter. She looked at her dressing table, and the passport was there, and it brought back the sharp pain. Freedom was an empty thing, a hollow shell if you loved someone, and they didn't love you. She closed her eyes. What utter madness to let herself fall for a man like Tor—an *adventurer*, a man so different from everything she had ever known as to be virtually of a race apart.

She sat down at the dressing table with its spotted mirror, and began to brush her hair. It was ridiculous, of course. Not love—merely infatuation for a very exciting, *very* experienced Slavic Romeo. And the sooner she was over it, the better. He would be back with his wife and children just as soon as he could. She brushed vigorously until tears of pain came to her eyes, put on a dash of lipstick—

and heard the rumblings of a car coming up the path.

. Quickly she ran to the window, ready to call Tor ... And she saw her own Citroën being driven slowly up the track towards the house.

Of course! He'd been for Madame Cassel! And she saw them getting out, saw Tor helping out the dumpy little woman she knew so well, almost as well as Tante Marie, lifting out her battered suit-case, and coming towards the house.

Sacha ran down to greet her, and flung her arms round the plump motherly figure and hugged her.

'Madame, it is so good to see you!'

'And you, my child. *Mais alors!* What has been happening?'

Tor was standing just inside the doorway with the case. He came forward, and said in French: 'I have been explaining to Madame the mix-up, and how it is now all sorted out, because we had an invitation to a friend's villa in Nice, and so all is well for you, Miss Donnelly.'

Sacha looked at him. It all came out so pat. But then he was used to telling lies. He had several years' start on them.

'But your bride, *m'sieur*, she is not here?'

He shrugged gracefully. 'She has gone on with our luggage. I have just a few personal things to collect, you understand. And then I too shall go. I wanted to be sure you were safely here before I left, to look after Miss Donnelly—and the hens, of course,' and he grinned boyishly, disarmingly, then

138

pointed to her case by the door. 'You will permit me to carry your case, *madame*? And I have your key.'

'Yes, yes, thank you. Such a surprise. I will return immediately, Sacha, to look after you.'

'Oh, no, *madame*, please don't trouble. Not this morning. I intend to have a few hours' painting, and there is really nothing I need.'

'*Comme vous voulez, ma chère.*' Madame Cassel was not displeased at having a morning in which to do her own work—and maybe to prepare some good excuses for letting down Sacha. She watched the old lady go with mixed feelings.

Tor returned a few minutes later, when Sacha was making her coffee in the kitchen. He stood in the doorway watching her for a moment, then said: 'Madame Cassel is back. I can leave.'

'Do you mean you wouldn't have gone if she hadn't returned today?'

'I would not have left you alone, no.'

'I'm really quite capable of looking after myself, Tor.' She would not turn round while she was speaking. She didn't want to see his face.

'That is not the point, I think. You expected her to be here when you came for a holiday—and now she is.'

Sacha turned round then. 'Yes. Even if it is a couple of days late. She's here. Have you things to get ready?'

'No. Everything is outside on my motorbike. And

here are your car keys. I put some *essence*—I mean petrol in, in Fréjus.' He came slowly forward from the doorway. 'Sacha, I want to see you again, please. May I come tomorrow?'

She looked at the car keys lying on the table. He had taken them from her, how long—three days ago? Was that *all*? It seemed an eternity. And now he was returning them, and it was all over.

'I thought you had to return home,' she said. If only he would *tell* her, it wouldn't be so bad. If only he would say——

'I am having some days' holiday first, in Cannes. I have nothing to hurry home for yet.'

Her heart went cold inside her. She picked up the car keys and dropped them in the pocket of her dress. Then speaking very carefully, for what she had to say was painful, she said:

'No, Tor, you may not come tomorrow, or the day after, or the day after that. I don't want to see you again.'

His face tightened. 'May I ask why?'

'Because it's all over. It's finished—all this——' she waved her hand. 'It's not real any more. They've gone—and now you can go, and I will have my holiday as I planned, on my own. You are not part of my plans. You weren't when I came, and you're not now.' It was an effort to speak. Tears stung her eyelids, but she fought for control, to stop them from falling. His face had gradually changed while she had been talking, and his eyes

. . . she wouldn't forget the expression in them for a long time.

She waited for him to answer, to argue, but he did neither. He just turned round and walked out of the kitchen. She heard the front door open, then close, and he passed the window. A minute later she watched him go down the track on his motor-bike. He didn't even look back once.

Sacha began to weep.

She didn't know how she got through the next few days. She painted, she drove down to the beach and went swimming, all the things she had intended to do—had been looking forward to doing on her own. But there was a deadly emptiness about everything, and reminders of Tor everywhere she went and in everything she did.

In another bedroom had been left an inch of after-shave in the bottom of the bottle, and Sacha had sniffed at it, and immediately been transported to that garden café in Cannes. That was what she had smelt that day, mingling with garlic and petrol. She put the bottle in the bottom of her suitcase so that she wouldn't forget it when the time came to leave.

Another two weeks to go, and she wondered if she would be able to bear it. Madame Cassel could not do enough to make up for her own 'defection', and kept dropping in excuses at every opportunity. Sacha longed to reassure her, to tell her that it didn't really matter, because nothing mattered any more. She was sleeping badly, waking to see that empty bed beside her with the moon casting its ghostly shadows, making it appear that someone slept there ... and she would weep, and pray for the holiday to end, because it had all gone so wrong, so very wrong.

The following Sunday she knew that she could take no more. She wanted to go home. Her father would welcome her with open arms, no questions asked, no inquest on what went wrong, no half-tactful hints.

Having decided, Sacha's heart was suddenly lighter. She ran up to her bedroom and packed, took her cases down to the hall and left a note saying she would be back soon, for Madame Cassel was due to come an hour or so later, and would wonder.

Sacha drove to the one place she wanted to go to just then—Tante Marie's. The door of the flat was ajar as usual, and she called: 'May I come in?'

'Of course. Sacha? My dear child, come in.' Tante Marie was dressed but not yet on her balcony. She sat in her chair near the window and held out her hand.

'What brings you so early on a Sunday? It is good to see you, my dear.'

There was a huge bowl of the most beautiful flowers on the table. As Sacha hugged her, Tante Marie said: 'See my pretty bouquet. From your lovely young man!'

Sacha jerked upright. 'W-what did you say?' Her face had gone ashen. Had she heard aright? Tante Marie saw, and frowned, and patted the chair beside her.

'Sit down, tell me what is the matter. Tell an old woman.'

Sacha obeyed, holding tightly to the wrinkled hand held out to her. 'Oh, Tante Marie, I'm going home. May I phone from here for a plane reservation?' And then the whole story came out, from the beginning with her arrival and first sight of Tor, through to her hearing from Wayne about his being married, to the final dreadful goodbye in the kitchen of the house. And the old woman, whose life had held its share of sorrow and trouble—and happiness—listened, and nodded, but didn't interrupt. She held tightly to Sacha's hand as if to give her strength to tell the tale.

When it was done, she sighed deeply. 'Oh, my dear, that it should have happened so. What can I say? And I liked him so much too—what a fine strong man, I thought—and a gentleman too. He had the manners of a prince, that one, and it is as natural to him as breathing. And see, these arrived a few days ago with a note.'

Sacha didn't want to, but she had to ask. 'What did it say?'

The old lady chuckled. 'He has a fine turn of phrase, that one, when he wants, I'll say that. "For the most beautiful woman in Cannes, with affection, Tor.' "He makes me feel not an old woman at all.'

Sacha smiled and bent to sniff the luxurious bouquet. In the centre of the many brightly coloured flowers was a perfect red rose.

'Beautiful.' She touched the rose. He had given her a rose too, and it was locked away for ever in glass. It would never fade or die as these blooms would in a short time.

She turned again to the old woman. 'So I'm going home. Dad won't ask questions. He never does. But I had to come and see you to tell you—so that you won't be disappointed if he—he—' she faltered, 'doesn't come to see you again.'

'No, my dear, I would not have been disappointed. At my age, one is past that. One lives for each day, and looks forward only to the next. And each day brings its own little surprises, believe me, Sacha. It will pass. It will pass, child.'

Sacha laid her cheek on the other's hand. 'I know. Thank you for listening. I knew you would understand, Tante Marie.'

She stayed there an hour or so longer, phoned Nice airport and got a cancellation on an evening flight that same day, and left after promising to write immediately she got home.

It was very late when the taxi drew up outside her house in a quiet tree-lined avenue. The lights were off, as she had expected, for she had been unable to get through from France on the phone.

Sacha let herself in and crept up to her father's bedroom, leaving her cases in the hall.

'Daddy, it's me, Sacha,' she said quietly. 'Are you asleep?'

'Wha—Sacha! Come in, I'm not asleep.'

She opened his door, and her father sat up in bed, his grey hair awry, pulling his glasses on from the bedside table. 'Good heavens, have I got all my dates wrong? I seemed to think——'

'No,' she went to drop a kiss on his cheek. 'No, you haven't got anything wrong. I just wanted to come home, that's all—and I came.'

He peered at her through his glasses. 'Ah, well, and here you are. You'll be hungry?'

She smiled. Her father rarely ate during the day when he was engrossed in painting, but at night she had known him sneak down past midnight for a furtive chicken sandwich and wedge of cake. 'A little,' she agreed. 'I was going to heat a tin of soup. You'll have some as well?'

'Ah, yes, good idea. I'll be down in a minute—just got to get my dressing gown on——'

She quietly went out and left him to wake fully, and went downstairs. She was glad to be home, in more ways than one. Tor and his kind had no place here, in the quiet ordered luxury of the detached home she and her father shared. John Donnelly was owner of a busy engineering works, left him by his father, Sacha's grandfather, a craggy old man she remembered only vaguely with respect tinged with fear. John had never wanted to go into busi-ness—his main love was painting, but he now managed to combine the two quite successfully, probably due to his happy-go-lucky personality and the affection he inspired in all his employees, shop stewards included. It was easy to like him, Sacha knew. And the factory had never had a strike in its seventy years of existence, which was probably a re-cord, for all she knew.

The kitchen was large, and the fluorescent lights sprang on, brilliantly illuminating everything in warm pink light. Bob the huge Irish wolfhound woke guiltily from his deep sleep curled up in the enormous basket in the corner by a radiator, stret-ched, yawned, and then, realising *who* it was, bounded over with a woof of pleasure.

Sacha knelt to hug him. 'And why didn't you wake up when I came in?' she asked him. 'Fine watchdog you are!'

He whined apologetically and wagged the tail that was long and furry enough to send a whole row of ornaments flying if he happened to be standing in the wrong place—and he frequently was.

Sacha threw him a biscuit and began to prepare their midnight snack. Sunday evening. In a few minutes it would be Monday. And just a week ago Tor had walked out of her life—literally walked out, just like that, without a word, without trying to talk her out of it, or argue. The memory of his face as he had looked just then haunted her. She stood still by the gleaming cooker for a moment, tin opener in hand, and it was as if she was back at that little house in France. He hadn't even said goodbye, just turned away and gone out of the door, and out of the house for ever. His face had been pale under his tan, and he had had a curiously blank expression, a shuttered, closed look, that did not reveal whether he was angry, whether in fact he cared at all. Perhaps he didn't.

She heard her father's footsteps, and quickly moved to open the tin of soup. 'I'll put plates out in a minute,' she said lightly. 'Sit down.'

Bob went to lay his head on John's knee, his long tail swishing the tiled floor, making a draught, and Sacha prepared the chicken soup and cut bread, and every action was mechanical. Tor had made soup, and he had worn shorts, and a tea towel tucked in at his waist . . . 'Stop it,' she thought, and didn't know she had spoken aloud until her father said mildly:

'Stop what?'

'Oh, nothing. Talking to myself.' She turned round to smile at him.

'Ah! Do it meself. Bad habit. Mrs. Brown thinks I'm going senile.'

'Never! She should get on with her work, then she wouldn't hear you.' Mrs. Brown came five days a week to housekeep and prepare her father's meals. The weekends were their own, and Sacha cooked then, and it was enjoyable, just the two of them, for they got on well, and if Sacha brought a boy-friend home, John Donnelly would get off to bed saying he was tired, and leave them downstairs on their own.

He knew about Nigel. He had never liked him, but had carefully avoided letting Sacha know, reckoning that it was none of his business. But it had been no surprise to him to hear that Nigel was married, and he was glad that Sacha had found out before she could be deeply hurt.

Now he watched her as she poured out the soup. Sacha could read his thoughts as well as if they were her own, and one day soon she would tell him most of what had happened at La Valaise—most—but not all. She hadn't told Tante Marie everything, had carefully avoided mention of Tor's kisses, of the way he had touched her, could send vibrations of longing surging through her—because some things are too personal ever to be said to anyone.

They drank their soup and ate the bread in warm companionable silence, then her father got up to fill a pan with milk. 'Might as well do it in style and round off the evening with cocoa,' he said. 'Not often we do this, eh?'

'No,' Sacha smiled. 'Not often.' Perhaps we will in future, she added inwardly. Because I've finished with men. Once bitten, twice shy, they said. And I've been bitten twice. I should have learned my lesson by now. And she put her hand to her head.

'Headache?' her father enquired.

'No, just tired. I think, if you don't mind, I'll take my cocoa upstairs and have it in bed.'

'Good idea. Off you go. I'll bring it up in a few minutes.'

She didn't see him watching her go out, didn't see the worried expression on his face. He knew that something had gone terribly wrong. But he would not ask, ever.

She had a week to go from work, and if she could have gone back, she would have done, but there would have been too much comment and speculation. It was only a small local paper, the staff were like a family, and everyone knew everybody else's business.

So Sacha got up late the following morning, and wondered just how she was going to spend the week. She could hear the vacuum cleaner humming away downstairs as she dressed in her beautiful bedroom with its blue and white decor, and the long white fitted wardrobes crammed full of her clothes. She put on a brown trouser suit with acid yellow silk tunic, for the weather was cooler. Then she went downstairs, prepared to parry Mrs. Brown's curious questions, for the woman knew she should have been away another week at least, and her mind would be buzzing with interesting

149

speculations.

Sacha breakfasted in the kitchen, coffee and toast, and knew her father would have gone to work. He always showed his face there on a Monday, and then got back to his painting. Where other managing directors sneaked off to golf and expense account lunches, he sneaked off home to the attic studio he had converted himself, and which nobody but Sacha was allowed to enter.

She took Bob for a walk, mainly to keep out of Mrs Brown's way, and also from cowardice. It was easier to avoid her than have a verbal battle of wits, for which Sacha felt she had no strength.

While out, she sent a telegram to Tante Marie to tell her she had arrived safely home, and would write, then she went into the park and sat on a bench while Bob chased pigeons vainly but ecstatically. She was beginning to rally round now that she was home. Her own strength of character was starting to assert itself again. She knew that there was no future in moping and wishing vainly for things better left behind, and forgotten.

So it was in a new frame of mind that she set off home eventually, after sitting for over an hour on a wooden park bench just thinking, going over everything, sorting out and getting her thoughts and emotions in some kind of order.

At lunch time she phoned her friend Janet, who was secretary to one of the town's solicitors. They had been friends since schooldays, were both the same age, twenty-two, had similar tastes in clothes, music and in their attitude to life.

'What on earth are you doing home? I've been watching the post for a card from you,' were Janet's first startled words down the line.

'It's a long story,' Sacha said lightly. 'But I'll tell you when I see you. That's what I've rung about. Are you doing anything tonight? There's a James Bond on I haven't seen.'

'Only going to wash my smalls,' was Janet's cheery reply. 'You're on. Can you call about six? Give me time to have a bite to eat.'

Sacha hung up thoughtfully after the call ended. Janet had been the best friend possible when she had found out about Nigel, not too curious, just *there*, with sympathy and a cool realism that had helped Sacha a lot. Should she tell her about Tor, and all that had happened? She didn't know. Perhaps she would when they met.

The film was escapist, exciting—and amusing in parts, and Sacha enjoyed herself more than she had imagined she could. After, they went to a local café and sat drinking coffee while Janet put Sacha up to date on all the latest gossip. She didn't ask any questions as to why the premature finish to the visit abroad. Perhaps she sensed something very wrong, and in the end, as they walked slowly home at half past ten, Sacha told her.

'Phew! Sacha!' Janet said softly when her friend

had finished. 'It's *incredible*. I mean, I know it's true because it's you telling me—but if I read it in a paper, I'd think it was someone's imagination working overtime.' Then she paused and added softly: 'This Tor. He sounds—fascinating. Does it hurt very much?'

Sacha nodded. 'Yes.' Her voice was husky and she had to clear her throat. 'Yes, it hurts like hell, Janet, but I'll get over it. I got over Nigel all right, didn't I?'

Janet nodded. 'Look,' she said hesitantly, 'I'm going to a party on Wednesday—no, wait——' this as Sacha opened her mouth. 'I know you don't want to go, I know you'll hate it, but you'll have to try, just for a little while, until it hurts a little less. You'll be welcome, honestly, and I'd love to go with you—we can have a good giggle, you know, like we always do—if nothing else, and anyway, I finished with Robert last week——'

'Oh, Janet, I'm sorry—why didn't you tell me before? Here's me rattling away about my troubles, and you keep quiet——'

Janet laughed. 'It doesn't matter. Honestly. He was getting too possessive, and all of a sudden I looked at him one day, and thought, oh, no! I don't fancy looking across a breakfast table at *you* all my life, so——' she shrugged lightly, 'we called off the romance quite amicably. He might even be at the party!'

'But you were going to get engaged on your

birthday——'

'Better to find out before it's too late, I always say. What about it, Sacha?'

'All right, thanks. I'll come. If you can recover, so can I. It'll stop me feeling so sorry for myself, won't it?'

They parted, and Sacha let herself into the house with her key, to be greeted by Bob. She had enjoyed her evening out, and now she had a party to look forward to, and if she carried on as she was doing, then perhaps in a week or so, the pain would be only a dull ache. Perhaps.

She had to force herself to get ready for the party on Wednesday evening. It was being held in the home of a friend of Janet's who lived several miles away, and the girls arranged to meet at Sacha's. Her father insisted on her going by taxi so that she would not have to drive home after drinking, and Sacha was quite agreeable. It was so rarely that he put his foot down, that she wouldn't refuse, and she knew too that it was sensible.

They set off at eight, and were soon there. At first Sacha had an unaccountably shy feeling at going into the warm bright room with its noisy crowd of young people dancing to the record player in the corner. She steeled herself to appear normal—she had never been like this before—looked round, and saw a preponderance of men, some of whom were already looking their way. She *would* have a good time, she decided. She jolly well *would*. She and Janet, both very attractive, were soon pounced on by two of the more good-looking members of the opposite sex, and to her surprise, Sacha found that it was quite possible to enjoy herself. Provided she didn't let herself think too much, that was. If she kept her mind very firmly off a certain house, and a certain man who had the power to turn her bones to water by a look or a touch, and who was so different from everyone there as to be almost like someone from another planet.

'I'm Nick, you're Sacha, and we've booked this next dance, I think.' There had been a temporary lull in the party. A lot of them had gone into another room to grab the food before it vanished, and Sacha had stayed behind to look at a huge pile of LPs because she wasn't a bit hungry. And this tall lean man bent over her, took her hand, and said his piece.

She looked up startled, then smiled, because she admired his cheek, and she liked that keen dark blue gaze that was very direct—and faintly admiring.

'Really? You mean they actually book dances at this party? I thought that went out with the valeta and feather boas.'

'Not at all,' he answered firmly, and put an old Frank Sinatra record on as if he owned the place— and maybe he did, for she wasn't sure just whose party it was. The music was dreamy, sentimental, and before she knew what was happening, Sacha was being steered round an almost deserted room, held very closely by this impudent young man who could not have been more than twenty-five, but who oozed self-confidence and a certain brash charm that appealed to her.

He took her out of the open french window and on to the darkened lawn before she could protest, and there he began to kiss her very firmly.

When he paused for breath, she said: 'Just a moment, whatever your name is, I don't——'

'Nick. It's Nick Jameson. I told you in there. Don't say you forgot!'

'Nick. Well, I have never——'

She wasn't allowed to finish. 'I know, that's your trouble. I mean, here am I, perfectly irresistible to women—and you've been ignoring me all evening!' He had his arm tightly round her.

'I've never even seen you——' and then, despite herself, she began to laugh. He really was incorrigible!

'That's better. Come on, let's go and get something to eat. I'm starving.'

Two hours later the party was beginning to break up, but Nick and Sacha, sitting talking in a corner, were barely aware of it. He was witty, a fascinating talker, and they were both getting on like a house on fire—only for Sacha it was simply someone to talk to. He might as well have been another girl for all the effect he had on her emotions.

'Can I run you home?' he asked with a quick look at his watch.

'Well, I came with Janet——' she peered round to see her friend in very close intimate conversation with a red-haired young man who looked as if he was trying to bite her ear off.

'Janet looks quite well taken care of, actually,' said Nick in dry tones. 'Still, we'll ask her. Okay?'

Janet looked round all starry-eyed and vague at Sacha's question. Sacha knew the look of old and went back to Nick, who stood up and grinned. 'Well?'

'She is, as you say, well taken care of,' said Sacha. 'But look—let's make something quite clear now. I——'

'I know. You don't need to tell me.'

'Tell you what?'

He smiled, and he was really very good-looking, but he could have been her brother for all the effect it had on Sacha. 'I must behave myself, not drive too fast, keep both hands on the wheel and not, repeat *not* run out of petrol on a deserted country lane.'

'Something like that,' she agreed. 'So if you don't feel like——'

'Then let's go. Cross my heart, I'll be perfect.'

He was as good as his word, and stopped outside Sacha's house twenty minutes later, and switched off. 'Right. When do I see you again?' he said.

'You don't. I mean—well, I've enjoyed this evening very much, but there's no point——'

'In going on. I see. Pining for someone else. Who is he? I'll punch his nose for him.'

Despite herself, Sacha had to smile. If only he knew! 'Something like that,' she admitted.

'Right, well, as long as we've got that straight—meet a man who's in the same boat, only in reverse, if you see what I mean.'

'You mean *you*——' she swallowed, hardly liking to go on.

'Yes. Me. Underneath this cheerful, idiotic exterior beats a broken heart. And now I've been honest—and I didn't intend to be, I confess, how about going out with me on a strictly platonic basis?'

'It sounds—all right. Yes. Thank you.' Sacha nodded.

'Good. Shake on it—or friendly platonic peck?'

'Friendly platonic peck if you like.'

His kiss was gentle and oddly comforting to Sacha. She watched him drive away after arranging to meet him two days later, Friday evening, to go out for dinner.

She went in and slept well for the first time in over a week.

He took her to a roadhouse several miles away on the Friday evening. You could eat and dance and drink, it didn't matter in what order, and it was a large place, and new, and Sacha found to her surprise that she was even managing to forget Tor for anything up to half an hour at a time. No longer than that.

And it was during their meal at the candlelit table that Nick told her his story. Sacha listened, glad in this small way to be of help, for it was obvious he needed to talk to someone, and the very fact of telling could in some way make the heartbreak less intense, as Sacha well knew.

He loved a girl, had been going out with her for nearly a year, but they had quarrelled a few weeks previously over something that was obviously important to them both. Sacha sensed, as she listened, that Nick was a very proud man, in spite of his bantering manner, and he was not prepared to accept the job offered to him by his girl-friend's father, a wealthy businessman.

The girl, Anne, could not understand his obstinacy, and the row had grown out of all proportion until they had had a blazing fight and parted. 'And that's it,' he said ruefully, stubbing a half-smoked cheroot into the glass ashtray. 'Anne thought I'd be delighted to work for her old man—at twice the money I'm getting now, of course. Whereas I intend to make *my* own way in life—and if she loved me enough, she'd see that. I'm not anyone's lapdog.'

'Couldn't you get together—just once—and talk it over?'

He gave her a wry look. 'I'm not going crawling

to her—and she's twice as pigheaded as I am—so?' he shrugged helplessly.

Sacha sighed. But she wasn't prepared to tell him about Tor and herself. Strange that both should share the same name. Tor was really Nikolai, although she had never thought of him like that.

'Come on,' Nick held out his hand. 'Let's dance, and make merry. I didn't come here to mope—and you know something? You're extremely sexy to dance with. If this wasn't a strictly platonic effort, I'd——' and he growled, and squeezed her. Sacha smiled. He was back to normal again. She only wished that there was some way in which she could help him. She didn't know how soon she would get the chance.

They had been at the party only half an hour when Sacha sensed that Nick had gone very withdrawn all of a sudden. It was the following night, Saturday, and he had persuaded her to go to a party with him. It was at a close friend's, he told her, and was guaranteed to be good. But he hadn't said that Anne would be going.

'She's here, isn't she?' Sacha said very quietly as they stood in a corner of the crowded room. She looked across to the hallway where a tall blonde girl stood watching them, and knew even before she asked the question that she was right.

'Yes,' Nick sounded wretched, 'but I swear I didn't know Mike would ask her—oh, *hell*!' he finished savagely. 'I can't stay here any longer—'

'Yes, you can,' Sacha answered calmly. She had seen the look on the blonde's face. Beautiful and serene she looked, but inside the yawning emptiness that Sacha recognised only too well. This Anne was in love with Nick, and if looks could kill, thought Sacha, I'd drop like a stone this minute.

She looked as though she would walk right out again, but someone took her arm, and dragged her in, and it was too late.

Each time Sacha danced past, with Nick, or someone else, she saw Anne's face, and her heart ached for her. She didn't know how lucky she was, thought Sacha wryly; she could get her romance put right, with a bit of a push. And then she had the idea. It might not work, and if it didn't Nick need never know—but she owed it to him to try, for in his own completely charming and friendly way he had helped her over the first few difficult days at home.

She waited for her chance, and when it came, she took it.

'Excuse me, Nick,' she gave him a sweet smile. 'But I must go and powder my nose. Won't be long,' and she pushed a plate of crisps on his knee and walked quickly upstairs. She had seen Anne go up, and she was timing it, praying that they wouldn't be interrupted.

It was perfect. As if planned. Anne went from the bathroom into the bedroom where all the

160

coats were, and Sacha followed her in. She shut the bedroom door behind her and Anne looked round startled, then, recognising her, a slow flush crept up her neck to her face.

'You don't know me,' Sacha said. 'But there's someone downstairs who loves you very much. His name's Nick.'

Anne stiffened and got up from the dressing table seat. Her eyes were very bright. 'I don't think——' she began.

Sacha didn't let her finish. 'Please listen,' she said. 'Because I want to help you. You see, I'm in love with a man, too—who doesn't love me. Nick and I met at a party this week and are going out together simply to have a shoulder each to cry on. I don't love him, and he doesn't love me, but I like him, and he's darned good company—and he's very unhappy—and I just thought I'd try and help him because'—she faltered for the first time—'because I know what it's like to love someone. It can hurt sometimes——' she blinked, because Tor's face was there, and words wouldn't come, and she suddenly realised how utterly stupidly she was behaving. She sat down on the bed. 'I'm sorry,' she said. 'It just seemed a good idea.'

'I'm sorry too,' said Anne, and sat beside her. 'I —I believe you. What's your name?'

'Sacha Donnelly.'

'Anne Carline.'

Suddenly they both smiled, and shook hands,

and it was different. Anne said very quietly: 'What shall I do?'

'Do you love him?'

'Yes.' She nodded. 'Oh, yes. I've been wretched since we split up. But when I saw you tonight——' she paused.

'I know.' Sacha pulled a little face. 'I *felt* it. Shall we go down?'

'W-what are you going to do?' asked Anne in a small voice.

'You'll see. Will you trust me, Anne?'

'Yes.'

They went into the packed living room and fought their way across. Nick's face was the study of a stunned man as he saw them arm in arm in front of him. He stood up slowly, and put the bowl of crisps very carefully down beside him.

'Anne,' said Sacha brightly, 'I'd like you to meet a friend of mine, Nick Jameson. Nick, this is Anne Carline, who'd love to join us.'

And suddenly she knew it had worked. It was in their eyes. There is no mistaking the eyes of someone when they see the one they love, she thought in wonder. It was all there, in the glow that came to Anne's, the tender, *loving* look in his. A look she might never be lucky enough to see—but what did it matter?

'I've just discovered I've got an awful headache,' she said. 'I'll go and phone for a taxi——'

'No, you're not.' Nick turned to Anne. 'All right

if we run Sacha home? It's too hot anyway in here.'

'Oh yes,' Anne agreed. 'It's much too hot.' And she smiled at him, and he smiled back at her, and Sacha felt a small warm glow.

'Look,' she said, 'would you both like to come in for a coffee?' It was nearly twelve, and the lights blazed out from her house, which was rather unusual because her father went to bed about ten—but perhaps he was waiting up.

Anne and Nick looked at one another, and smiled. He shook his head. 'Thanks, Sacha, but not tonight. We have a few things to talk about, and it's late.' He turned round to her. 'But thanks—for everything.'

'Thank *you*,' she answered. 'You helped me as well, when I needed it—I shall miss going out with you——' and then, hurriedly to Anne, because she knew it sounded odd: '—I mean that in the nicest possible way, believe me.'

'I know you do.' Anne positively glowed. Even in the car, with only the dim interior light on, she had a radiance about her. 'I know, Sacha. Thank you too.'

Nick got out to open the back door and help Sacha out. As he did so he whispered: 'And we'll send you an invite to the wedding.'

'I'll keep you to that.' She smiled at him. ' 'Bye, both of you. I'll be seeing you.' But she didn't know, couldn't imagine just then when she *would* next see them.

She ran up the path and waved as they drove off, then with a sigh, opened the door. The first thing she heard were men's voices from the kitchen, then Bob dashed out with a welcoming deep-throated bark, and she heard her father say: 'Ah, there she is now. Early. I wasn't expecting her back just—' and she walked slowly to the kitchen, because something was building up inside her. It was as if she knew whom she would see. Then she was in the doorway, and a man standing by the cooker turned round and looked at her.

The man was Tor.

CHAPTER SEVEN

SACHA had to hold on tightly to the door to stop
herself from falling.

'Hello, Sacha,' said Tor quietly.

'Hello.' And she stayed where she was. The men
had been making coffee. The scene was imprinted
on Sacha's brain so vividly that she knew she would
never forget it.

Tor was dressed so differently, in dark blue
blazer and grey trousers, white shirt and tie. Vital
and virile-looking, a tall very handsome man whose
presence sent the blood pounding in her head.

She heard her father say vaguely: 'If you'll excuse me a moment—I must just . . .' and he wan-
dered out—but it didn't register, none of it did,
not even when her father was calling for Bob to go
with him—and then Sacha and Tor were alone.

And she found her voice. 'How—how did you
get here?' she spoke huskily, and she couldn't do
anything about it, because she was fighting to keep
on her feet, and she was *not* going to faint.

'I flew to London, and then caught a train,' he
answered. 'Because yesterday I went to see Tante
Marie, and spent most of the day with her—and
after I left her I went to Nice Airport to book a
flight, but the first one I could get was today's.' He

came forward, and Sacha said:

'Please don't come any nearer.' She couldn't take it in—but she didn't know what she would do if he touched her, because her defences were perilously weak, and the only place she wanted to be was in his arms—but he must never know.

'If you think,' he said, 'that I have come many miles to be sent away again, you are mistaken. Why did you not tell me at La Valaise just *why* you didn't want to see me again?' His accent was carefully controlled, and he spoke slowly as if everything he said was of great importance, and must be understood.

She took a deep breath. 'Surely you must know? Was it necessary for me to spell it out? I do *not* go out with married men——'

'But I am not married, Sacha.'

She shook her head. Contempt curled her lip. 'I know that lying comes easily to you,' she said. 'It's part of your job, isn't it? But to deny your wife and children——'

'She is my sister, and I am the children's uncle,' he cut in. 'I swear that most solemnly to you now, on the memory of my mother. I am not married, I have never been married and I have no children.'

'I—I don't——' Sacha felt as if she was going to faint. She reached out her hand, and then Tor was by her side, and she wasn't trying to fight him any more. For the first time ever, when he put his arm round her, she turned to him and let herself relax, and he kissed her, and again, until they both trembled, and he drew away, his eyes dark with love, and looked at her and breathed: 'Sacha, *dushinka*, do you not know that I love you with all my heart? I have suffered as no man should have to suffer since that day—that terrible day that you sent me away.'

They had moved. Sacha was leaning against the cupboards, with Tor so close that she couldn't stir —but she didn't want to. She wanted to be there, right there, with his arms tightly round her, as they were, and never have to move away.

'I love you too,' she whispered. 'And you're not the only one who's been miserable—but how—why —Wayne told me——'

'Wayne was telling the truth—as he knew it. If only I had known, while we were all there! I sensed you were different when you were back from your walk with him, and I gave you that little present, but I did not know why. And when, that next morning, you told me you did not wish to see me again, my pride would not allow me to plead. I do not crawl, ever, to anyone.'

He tilted his head back, and Sacha saw a trace of that arrogant assurance, and smiled. She lifted her hand and gently traced a finger down his cheek.

Tor groaned and brushed her forehead with his lips. 'Don't do that, *dushinka*,' he whispered. 'You do not know what you are doing to me.'

Sacha laughed softly, her heart bursting with

happiness, and he went on: 'When Anna, my sister and I defected, several years ago, we had to pose as man and wife—and somehow, I suppose, Wayne heard that, and never learned different afterwards. Anna got married soon after, to a French Naval officer, and we became partners in a very busy restaurant. But now her husband is leaving the Navy, and I am thinking of selling my share to him. They have a son and a daughter too—oh yes, and a cat called Minou who catches mice. I am thirty-three —a very old man, I am afraid—and I like cooking best of all—no, not best of all. Best of all is making love to you, which I will be doing very soon.' And he laughed.

When they managed to tear themselves apart, and Sacha had spent a moment wondering vaguely where her father had gone, she made coffee for them both and they sat at the kitchen table, holding hands across the red formica top.

'Why did you go to see Tante Marie?' she remembered to ask.

'Because I had promised to—and I was ready to go back home.' He stroked Sacha's wrist gently. 'It is due to her that I am here, for she told me that you loved me——' he laughed at Sacha's startled exclamation. 'Yes, she did. She is a very wise old lady, your Tante Marie. And then she told me *why* you had sent me away—and there was a look in her eyes that frightened me!'

He paused to drink his coffee, and Sacha watched

him, her eyes brimming with happiness.

Every inch of his face was remembered, had been with her constantly all through the days of loneliness since her departure from La Valaise, every line and plane was etched for ever in her brain. And now he was with her. And that was all that would ever matter.

'So I told her what I have just told you—that I have never been married—and it was now becoming clear to me also that I had been very stupid. I said that I would go to La Valaise immediately— and I was half way out of her apartment before she could tell me that you had left, gone home.' He closed his eyes and lifted her hand to his face, there to kiss it. 'You do not know how I felt then—I cannot tell you—but Tante Marie made me sit down and made me drink my wine, and she began to tell me all about you—but I already knew. Oh, Sacha, she did not need to tell me anything, for I feel as if I have known you all my life. When we were at the house—when I was having to be so cruel to you, and keep you there, I hated myself. It hurts me to be unkind to a woman. I hated myself. I was terrible to you, I know. Will you find it in your heart to forgive me?'

'There is nothing to forgive,' she answered simply. 'Nothing—ever. Perhaps it is a good thing that this—separation has happened. I know now that I can't live without you——' she stopped.

'How soon can we be married?' he said. 'Can it

be tomorrow?' His grey eyes were dancing.

She laughed. 'Oh, Tor! Tomorrow! I wish it could.' And she honestly couldn't remember how it was that she was no longer on her own chair, but sitting on his knee.

A month later they became man and wife in the little church at the end of Sacha's road. It was a simple ceremony, with only relatives and close friends, and Janet was Sacha's bridesmaid.

Tor's best man was his French brother-in-law, Paul, who flew over especially for the ceremony.

Outside the church afterwards, as they posed for the photographer, Sacha saw a radiant Anne standing with Nick. She had said she would see them again—but never in all her wildest imaginings could she have imagined it would be there. They waved, and Sacha caught the glitter of a diamond on Anne's finger, and turned to smile at her new husband. Some day she would tell him about them. There was so much to talk about, to discover, though first, much more important, she wanted to learn about Tor's life before they met. She already knew it would be fascinating, that she had married a man who was rare—and the thought that he loved her as much as she did him was too wonderful for any words.

There was one person who could not be at the wedding; someone they would both have loved to be there above all others. Tante Marie was too old to travel. But she was going to have a surprise very shortly.

Sacha and Tor flew to Paris for two days—and nights—and after hiring a car, drove down the N7 —the main route to the south, calling at Tor's restaurant on the way, where a superb meal was waiting for them, together with his beautiful dark-eyed sister, her husband and their two children, Paul and Maria.

Sacha knew that her cup of happiness was brimming over, but the best was yet to come.

The night after their visit to her new in-laws, they stayed at the Carlton in Cannes. Sacha lay in bed and turned to look at the sleeping man beside her. The moonlight came through the fine net curtains at the window and fell on him, and it was so much like the other times at La Valaise that she put out her hand to touch him to make sure he was real. He stirred slightly in his sleep, and murmured: 'Sacha, *dushinka*,' and she smiled to herself. He was teaching her Russian, and she knew her first word very well—*dushinka*, darling. And there were others too, words of love, that she was learning, with all the other things he was teaching her, too private and wonderful to be told.

In the morning they breakfasted on the balcony of their room.

'You think she will be surprised to see us?' Tor asked, buttering a flaky warm *croissant* to pass to his new wife.

'Yes. And it's thanks to her that we're here at all,' she answered. 'We owe Tante Marie a lot.'

They set off in their hired car, and she was waiting on her balcony, just as if she had known they would be coming. She waved, and called to them, tears coursing down her cheeks. 'My dears, come on up—ah, this is so marvellous!'

But Tante Marie had to wait. The lift was out of order—again—and the dark stairways were too much temptation for Sacha and Tor, who found it necessary—and exciting—to kiss at every shadowy corner on that long walk up.

And then, when eventually they were there, Tante Marie had made her slow way to the door to greet them.

'I don't know what you've been doing,' she grumbled, 'but it's taken you ages to climb those stairs.' But there was a twinkle in her eyes as she drew them into the apartment, and perhaps there were memories too.

Romance is Beautiful

Get to the HEART OF HARLEQUIN

HARLEQUIN READER SERVICE is your passport to The Heart of Harlequin . . .

if You...

 enjoy the mystery and adventure of romance then you should know that Harlequin is the World's leading publisher of Romantic Fiction novels.

 want to keep up to date on all of our new releases, eight brand new Romances and four Harlequin Presents, each month.

 are interested in valuable re-issues of best-selling back titles.

 are intrigued by exciting, money-saving jumbo volumes.

 would like to enjoy North America's unique monthly Magazine "Harlequin" — available **ONLY** through Harlequin Reader Service.

are excited by **anything new** under the Harlequin sun.

then...

YOU should be on the Harlequin Reader Service — **INFORMATION PLEASE** list — it costs you nothing to receive our news bulletins and intriguing brochures. Please turn page for news of an **EXCITING FREE OFFER.**

a Special Offer for You...

just by requesting information on Harlequin Reader Service with absolutely no obligation, we will send you a "limited edition" copy, with a new, exciting and distinctive cover design — **VIOLET WINSPEAR'S** first Harlequin Best-Seller

LUCIFER'S ANGEL

You will be fascinated with this explosive story of the fast-moving, hard-living world of Hollywood in the 50's. It's an unforgettable tale of an innocent young girl who meets and marries a dynamic but ruthless movie producer. It's a gripping novel combining excitement, intrigue, mystery and romance.

A complimentary copy is waiting for YOU — just fill out the coupon on the next page and send it to us to-day.